Justifiable Deception

~ ~ ~ *Kelly Lewis* ~ ~ ~

Justifiable Deception

Justifiable Deception
Copyright 2020 by Kelly Lewis Haggmark
ISBN 978-1-79486-744-4

No part of this publication may be reproduced, stored in a retrieval system or transmitted in any way by any means, electronic, mechanical, photocopy, recording or otherwise without the prior permission of the author except as provided by USA copyright law.

Cover Design by Jake Haggmark
Cover Photography by Lindsay Banerjee

For Ellice

Special thanks to:

Colleen Lewis
Jake Haggmark
Kathy Lewis
Lindsay Banerjee
Trish O'Keefe
Rick Haggmark

Prologue

Part One – William

Part Two – Layton

Part Three – Ellie

Part Four - Discovery

Prologue

Mitch entered the office and sat in the chair next to Bobby's desk. Bobby was smoking a cigar, reading the paper.

"Hey Pops, what's up?" Mitch asked.

"Have one," Bobby said as he opened the cigar box on his desk and pushed it towards Mitch. "Let's have a drink?"

"Sure, I'll get 'em. Scotch?"

"Yeah, whatever."

"So what's goin' on? You said you needed to talk," Mitch said as he poured their drinks.

"We got a problem, and I need you to take care of it."

"K. Who is it now?"

"Lou."

"What's he done? Skimmed a little from the books?"

"Nah. He wants to quit. Says he doesn't want to stay in the game. Thing is, he seems spooked, and I can't trust him."

"Think it's that bad?"

"Yup," Bobby replied.

"What ya want done?"

"We gotta get rid of him. Can't risk the feds gettin' hold a him."

"But he's family," Mitch exclaimed. Bobby paused and dragged on his cigar.

"Right, but family or not, if we can't trust him, he's done. So we gotta get rid of him."

"Okay, I'll take care of it."

"Make sure it's clean."

"I will, don't worry 'bout it." Mitch got up to refresh their drinks then asked, "who's gonna do the books after he's gone."

"I think I should get someone legit, a CPA type."

"You think that's a good idea?" Mitch asked.

"Sure. I'll get someone young, maybe a guy with a family. I'll keep him happy, string him along, and bring him into the family when the time is right."

Part One

William

Chapter One

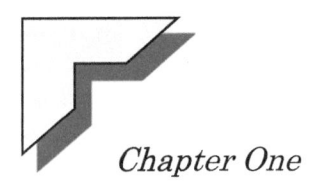

William Gable stepped out of his car after pulling into the parking garage near his office. It was Friday morning, and he was looking forward to the weekend spending time with his wife, Suzanne, and baby daughter, Ellie. They were going to have a picnic in the park on Saturday and then Sunday dinner with his mother, Eleanor.

As he turned away from his car, he nearly ran into a man in a dark suit. It caught him off guard. He hadn't seen the man when he drove into his parking spot.

"Oh, excuse me," William said. "I didn't see you there. Is there something I can do for you?"

The man in the suit moved in closer and discreetly opened a leather folder holding his identification on one side and a badge on the other.

"Agent Matthew Breene, FBI. Are you William Gable?" His voice was low but intense. His gaze shifted past William and then from side to side as they carried on this brief conversation.

"Yes, I'm William Gable. What do you want?"

"We need to speak to you, in private, away from your office. Can you come with us now?"

"No, I don't think I can. I have a meeting at nine o'clock with my boss. Am I in any trouble?" William asked.

The FBI man answered, "No, no trouble, we have some questions for you. There's nothing for you to be concerned about. It's just a routine matter. We understand this isn't a good time. We'll be in touch....soon."

And with that he lifted his arm motioning toward the back corner of the garage. A black SUV pulled up, and the agent jumped into the front passenger seat. The vehicle quickly drove away leaving William dazed and confused.

William worked for Homeward Enterprises, a family-owned construction business. He was a certified public accountant and their chief financial officer. At first, he believed this was his dream-come-true job offered to him at a time in his career and personal life when he was unhappy working in the field of public accounting.

After graduating from college, he went to work for a local CPA firm. Having passed the CPA exam at his first sitting, he put in the two years needed to become certified and early on was recognized for his talent and competence in the firm. Unfortunately, that recognition led to a substantial client load, long hours, and ever-increasing responsibilities. It wasn't that he couldn't handle it. He understood this all meant he was beginning a successful career, and partner in the firm would surely be the reward yet it seemed to be coming too fast, too soon.

At the time, he was newly married hoping to start a family right away and, as much as he wanted success in his career, he knew that came with a price. He worried about his wife and children becoming lost under the umbrella of his success, and he didn't want to miss too many of the important moments.

Along came Homeward Enterprises with an offer he couldn't refuse. The move from public accounting would mean a standard nine to five, Monday through Friday work week. He knew there would be occasional overtime, but nothing compared to tax season at the firm. From January through April each year he worked sixteen hour days including Saturdays and, as the April fifteenth deadline approached, Sundays as well. After tax season ended, a brief lull gave them time to catch their breath and then what they called the second tax season began with the filing deadline in October for returns where extensions had been filed.

It was difficult enough with a wife at home, but the thought of going through that grueling schedule year after year while raising children just left a pit in his stomach that he couldn't ignore. He enjoyed his work, but also believed there had to be a way to pursue a rewarding career without sacrificing too much of his personal life. He had hoped to find the right balance and Homeward offered him that opportunity.

The Company was owned by Robert (Bobby) Renaldi, a man in his early sixties. He had three sons, and they all worked for the business. Homeward specialized in affordable housing projects, and they were growing as they expanded all over the state. Most of their projects received state grants and affordable housing funding because they dedicated a minimum number of units for residents in low-income categories.

Bobby's cousin had handled the bookkeeping, but he wanted to retire and move to Florida. When William first talked with Bobby about the job he learned that the business was getting too big for his cousin to handle and he felt it was time to hire an accountant. A certified public accountant was what Bobby said the job needed and William jumped at the chance to get out of public accounting.

The next few years were good. He enjoyed the job, and he and Suzanne welcomed their first child into the family. As he worked at Homeward, he learned that working for a private company was different from public accounting. Public accounting had its own set of drawbacks such as juggling multiple and diverse clients, long hours, and pressure to accumulate billable hours. He didn't miss that at all and enjoyed getting out of work each day at five and his free weekends felt like mini vacations.

The only problem was William felt he was underutilized, not able to use many of his skills. Bobby kept a lot of his business dealings private, sharing only with his three sons. William quickly learned he was working under a need-to-know basis and there were times he doubted all of Bobby's business practices were legal and ethical.

It wasn't that he had any proof that Bobby was doing anything wrong, but he felt a little troubled about the fact that he was not involved in the process of securing state grants, affordable housing funding, and government contracts. As Bobby's financial guy, he thought he would be a big part of the bidding process providing guidance and financial information.

When William questioned him about it, Bobby just replied, "Don't worry Billy, we have ways of cuttin' through the red tape. You just deposit the checks when they start rolling in and hey, maybe a nice bonus for you this year."

This made William skeptical, but he pushed the feelings aside because the job afforded him the ability to find that work-life balance that he so desperately desired.

Bobby was the only person who called William Billy. He hated it, but William put up with it because he was a little intimidated by his boss and thought it best not to make an issue of it.

Today his meeting was with Bobby and his three sons. William was uneasy about it because it was rare for him to be included. The earlier conversation with the FBI agent was also in the back of his mind, adding to his uneasiness. At the same time, he wondered if the meeting with Bobby meant he was going to be brought into his confidence, moving into a position of greater trust after working diligently for the past few years. He was eager and anxious at the same time about the meeting. Deep down he hoped he would soon be able to sink his teeth into some real accounting work instead of the usual glorified bookkeeping tasks.

After dropping his coat and briefcase off at his office, he got himself a cup of coffee and went to the conference room. Bobby and his sons, Joey, Sam, and Mitch, were already there seated around the table. The mood was a bit chilly. He was never actually comfortable around Bobby's boys. He felt like an outsider and with good reason, he was the only nonfamily member working in the office.

Bobby started, "Billy, come in, have a seat. We got somethin' we need to talk to you about." William sat down after making polite greetings to each of the sons. He immediately realized his anxious anticipation of the meeting was the right one. He could see it in their faces.

"What's going on, Bobby? Is anything wrong?" William asked.

"No, no, Billy. Listen, ya know we've been in business a long time, and we do pretty good, right? You see tha numbers." William thought he was expected to respond, but when he started to speak, Bobby put up his hand in a motion to stop him and then continued.

"Here's tha thing, I wanted to get us all together to, you know, discuss a few things." Bobby hesitated, and William saw for the first time concern in his eyes, and this was uncharacteristic. Bobby was always upbeat, flashing a smile, patting you on the back, and he was very generous with his business profits both to employees and the community. Something was wrong, William could feel it.

"So Billy, here's what we gotta go over. Ya know we get a lot a government dough for our housing projects, but it's competitive, and some guys get a bug up their butt when they don't get the same incentives. Now it seems we're gettin' looked at .... sort of under suspicion. You might be seeing somethin' in the news soon about us being favored when the government's doling out funds. We're all on the up an' up, but rumors start, and I wanted to give ya a heads up."

"Wow, Bobby, that's too bad. Do you think it's serious? I mean, we don't have anything to worry about, right?"

Bobby looked William straight in the eye with conviction and replied, "Course not, nothing to worry 'bout. It'll all go away in a few weeks, but we should get some things straight. We all need to be careful about what we say. We got our lawyers handling the whole situation."

"That's good," William replied.

"So Billy, remember, you don't need to say anything and don't share any documents or financial stuff with anyone. If anything comes up, come to me and let me know. Gotta work with our lawyers in situations like this."

William paused as he took it all in for a few moments. His mind flashed back to the FBI man this morning, and he briefly considered telling Bobby about it. He decided against it and then replied, "Alright, Bobby, I understand. I'll be aware. Honestly, I wouldn't have much to share anyway since I've never been involved in the bidding process, and I never understood why you didn't need me to...."

Bobby interrupted, rising from his chair, "That's about all we needed to talk about. I don't want to keep ya from your work. Thanks for comin' in."

William took that as a directive to leave as Bobby clearly had no more to say on the subject.

Back in his office, William sat at his desk unable to focus on his work. The day had started out on his drive in with happy anticipation of the weekend ahead, and now his mind was spinning from what had happened in the course of one hour. He didn't know what to make of it. First the FBI and then Bobby's meeting. Something was going on, and he was totally in the dark.

The FBI must know he's the company accountant and they think he can give them information. Nothing could be further from the truth. William was just a numbers man, and he was not in the know. He started to sweat. He needed to think. So many thoughts were reeling in his head.

Bobby did seem to get a lot of funding awarded to his projects and with ease. Some of their projects were government-owned housing developments for seniors and low-income families where Homeward submitted a bid to construct the buildings. Then there were projects Homeward built, owned, and rented with sections designated for low-income individuals and families. They had to meet specific requirements to secure subsidies, tax breaks, and other financial incentives.

William believed Bobby was a smart businessman taking advantage of what the government had to offer and it was working as evidenced by the growth of the company.

He hadn't seen anything suspicious in his work at Homeward, but at times he doubted Bobby was completely above board. He and his sons seemed to live pretty well, and William felt his salary was on the high side including generous annual bonuses.

He remembered a time when he wanted to sit down with Bobby and talk about some business details. Bobby's response was, *don't ask questions, I'll tell ya whatcha need to know when ya need ta know.* This attitude of Bobby's made William wonder why Bobby hired a CPA in the first place if he wasn't going to let him put his knowledge and experience to work.

He felt like a taskmaster just paying the bills and issuing invoices. And when it came time to file their income taxes, he wasn't involved at all. That was especially strange since William was well versed in the area of business tax law.

Then there was the firm that Bobby used to handle all of their tax work. It was small, without a good reputation. After William had been working for Bobby for several months, he ran into one of the partners from the CPA firm he previously worked for and asked him about Bobby's choice in accounting firms. The response he received was - *be careful, William, I would hate to see you mixed up in something that would harm your career.* When William asked him to elaborate, the man clammed up causing William to question his decision to leave the firm. Had he been too hasty in accepting the position with Homeward? In hindsight, he thought maybe he should have checked them out more thoroughly, but his initial research gave him no indication the company was anything but solid, and when he accepted the offer, he felt it was a good move for him.

Now, for today, William needed to try to put things out of his mind and get back to work. He would keep himself busy for the rest of the day, maybe talk about it with Suzanne this evening over a glass of wine, and then he would sleep on it.

As the end of the day approached, he hoped there would be no FBI presence when he left the office. William didn't think he could handle another encounter just yet. He needed some time to mull things over before talking to them, and now that Bobby was on guard, he didn't want to risk being seen talking to the FBI.

Chapter Two

"How's my big girl doing today?" William asked as he scooped up Ellie after coming in the front door.

"Daddy! Daddy, home," she said with a squeal followed by a giggle as he nuzzled into her neck.

"Oh, how I missed my Ellie today. What would you like to do while momma cooks dinner? Want to have a horsey ride or how about a book read? Anything you want tonight."

"Horsey ride, horsey ride."

And with that, he got down on his hands and knees and helped her climb onto his back. He flipped his tie to the back, she grabbed on to it like reins, and off he went bopping along and whinnying from the front door to the kitchen.

William was a serious accountant by day, but a fun-loving father when the workday was done. Even with the events of the day still weighing on his mind, he didn't want his little girl, just fifteen months old, to sense anything out of the ordinary in her innocent world.

Suzanne was busy at the kitchen island mixing up a salad. She greeted William with a smile and said, "Happy Friday!" After getting up off the floor, William picked up

Ellie, gave Suzanne a kiss and echoed "Happy Friday" with a high five.

Dinner was typical with Ellie banging her spoon on the highchair tray and William feeding her with all the motions and sounds of various modes of transportation including trains, airplanes, and racecars. After dinner, Suzanne cleaned up the kitchen, and William gave Ellie her nightly bath. They worked through their bedtime routine, and she was off to sleep shortly after 7:30.

Before leaving the nursery, William took a few moments to watch his little girl sleep. He thought about how happy he was the day she was born and each day since brought so much joy watching her grow. It was good to pause and take in this quiet moment, but as he suddenly became overwhelmed and thought he would shed a tear, he quickly closed the door and proceeded down the stairs.

Being Friday night, William and Suzanne settled down on the living room sofa with a bottle of Merlot and soft jazz playing in the background. This was their time to unwind and talk about the events of the week without any interruption from their very active one year old daughter. Suzanne was thrilled to have adult conversation, and she was never at a loss for words once she began.

After filling William in on all that she and Ellie had done during the week, she stopped to give him a chance to talk about his week, but he sat quietly looking deep in thought. She felt something was off.

"Hey there, are you with me?" She asked as she waved her hand in front of his face.

"Oh sorry, Suz. I've got something on my mind because of what happened at work today. I wasn't sure when to tell you about it. I hate to ruin our evening."

"William, you need to tell me because it's obviously bothering you. Don't worry about ruining our evening, that's what this time is for – good or bad to talk things out. So fill me in. What happened?"

William proceeded to tell her about the visit from the FBI and then the meeting at the office with Bobby.

"That's so bizarre. Something must be going on. The FBI agent didn't say when they would talk to you again?" Suzanne asked.

"No. He just said soon. I was worried he would find me after work, but there was no sign of him. I feel like I need time to think, maybe even see if I can find something more out at work before I talk to them. The FBI must think I know something."

"Although, it might not even be something about work, right? They didn't ask you anything about Homeward, did they? And they didn't tell you not to say anything about it."

"No, that's true they didn't. I just assumed it has to be something to do with the company I work for since that's where they stopped me, and then that meeting with Bobby was oddly coincidental."

"It does seem odd."

"And you know, sometimes I'm not so sure about Bobby and his business."

Suzanne looked confused and replied, "Wait. You think something illegal might be going on?"

"No, not really," he said with a shrug.

"You've never said you suspected anything before. I always assumed everything was great at work. I mean it's been so nice to have you here more, and you seem to enjoy working there. I know Bobby isn't the perfect boss, but am I wrong, haven't you been happy at Homeward?"

"Yes, for the most part, things have been fine, but I've had a feeling now and then that Bobby draws the line on legal and ethical issues in a different place than I would."

"What do you mean, William?"

"It's not that there's anything I know about. Honestly, Bobby keeps me in the dark on a lot of things. I just do accounting transaction work. I'm not privy to anything related to how the business is run or what goes into any decisions being made." He took a drink of wine thinking before continuing. "There is one thing that has always bothered me."

"What's that?"

"How quickly we seem to be awarded government contracts and funding. Then the fact that I'm never called upon to prepare any information for the submission of bids. It's weird because I have so much experience pulling together and presenting financial information. I did a great deal of that type of work for our clients at the firm. When Bobby hired me, I thought it was because of that experience and that I would be heavily involved in most business deals."

"I didn't realize, but I'm a little surprised you haven't shared this with me before now. Has it been a concern for you?"

William sighed as he responded, "Not really. And I'm sorry I haven't talked about it before. It was just a minor thing, something I would avoid thinking about. I loved the hours, and the work is easy, money's good."

"Right on all points."

"I've been so happy with my personal life with you and Ellie that I told myself I didn't care what Bobby did with his business as long as I did what was expected of me and could walk away when the day was done."

"I can understand that. You're just his employee doing what you're told to do, and you haven't actually witnessed anything illegal, but now I believe your gut feeling may be right that something is going on."

"Maybe," he said with a pensive look.

"I'm thinking it may be a good thing that Bobby doesn't share much with you. That way, you won't have anything to tell the FBI."

She then stood up and paced in front of the coffee table and continued, "that's right, William. I'm on to something here. I don't think you should try to find out anything. I think you should just tell the FBI you don't know anything, which is the truth. That way they will just leave you alone."

She sat back down feeling satisfied with her assessment of the situation, but William wasn't convinced.

"It sounds good, in theory, but I'm not sure the FBI will leave me alone simply because I say I don't know anything. Maybe they won't believe me. If something *is* going on, they may think I'm lying."

"You're right, they might, but aren't we getting ahead of ourselves? We don't even know what it's all about yet."

William poured them each a little more Merlot and said, "Right, we are getting ahead of ourselves, and I think I'm done talking about this."

"Me too!" Suzanne stated.

"I'll just wait until the FBI contacts me again and see what they have to say." They clinked glasses, smiled, and took a drink. The rest of the evening was filled with ease, and William was able to put the events of the day out of his mind...for now.

Chapter Three

William awoke early Saturday morning and started preparing their usual breakfast, blueberry pancakes with lots of maple syrup. The house was quiet with Suzanne and Ellie still asleep giving him a little time to himself. He enjoyed his first cup of coffee in peace.

After mixing up the pancake batter, he sat looking out the patio door from the morning room table sipping his coffee and thinking about the day before. Last night he worked hard to put the conversation with the FBI agent out of his mind, but now, alone with his thoughts, he began to panic. *What could they possibly want with me? When will they contact me? They said they would be in touch soon.*

William had always been one to follow the rules. He was a good student all through school and college and, as a CPA, he performed his work with the highest ethical standards.

Clients were not always on the same page. From keeping two sets of books - one hiding revenues, to trying to take deductions for nondeductible expenses, to transacting business under the table, some companies tried to minimize federal and state taxes illegally. There were times when his firm was forced to discontinue working with a client because they were unwilling to do things required by law. Fraud and tax evasion were serious crimes, and certified public accountants have a responsibility to educate clients and ensure businesses are compliant with respect to those laws and regulations.

Now to think he may be involved with the kind of company his former employer would not work with, that was unsettling. He always believed the accountants that knowingly serviced clients engaged in illegal activities were every bit as guilty as the client.

He had performed several audits over the years, and there were instances when his testing led to suspicion of illegal activities. At that point, he would supply his documentation with an audit summary to the board of directors, and they would take it from there. His role in the process was to review financial records and report his findings giving an opinion based on his audit testing.

His thoughts were interrupted as his wife entered the room carrying his baby girl, both all smiles. The kitchen became all a flurry with conversation and laughter as they prepared breakfast and sat down to eat. After the dishes were done and put away, they dressed and packed the things they needed for their day at the park including a picnic lunch.

The park was about thirty minutes away, and it was a perfect day for a family outing. While Suzanne was busy setting up the picnic table, William took Ellie to the playground where she enjoyed her favorite swings. Not long after he set her in the swing and started giving her a few gentle pushes, he noticed a man walking towards him. It was odd because you didn't typically see anyone at the playground without a child. As the man approached, he could see it was Agent Breene.

"Mr. Gable."

"Yes?"

"I'm sorry to bother you on the weekend, but can we talk for a few minutes?"

"Okay. Let me bring my daughter over to my wife so we can talk alone."

William took Ellie out of the swing and brought her over to Suzanne. He explained that the FBI agent was here and he would talk to him for just a little while hoping to learn more about what was going on.

After returning to the playground, he asked Agent Breene if they could sit on one of the park benches in the distance and the Agent agreed.

William began, "Before we get started, I just have one question. How did you know I was here?"

"That's not important right now. What is important is that we need to speak with you and since we couldn't talk yesterday, I thought it would be better to see you away from the office. This seemed like the best opportunity."

"Well, I suppose," William replied totally dissatisfied with the Agent's answer. "So what is it you want with me?"

"It's information we need."

"What kind of information, about what?"

"Homeward Enterprises."

"Okay. What about them? I don't seriously think there's any information I can give you."

"They are currently under investigation, and as their accountant, we believe you may be able to help us. We understand you are one of the few employees without family ties. Is that right?"

"Yes, that's right. I'm not related to anyone in the company, but most everyone else is part of the family, at least among those that work in the office."

"Good, that helps."

"But honestly, that could prove to be a problem. You see since I'm not in the family, they don't share much with me. I basically do the bookwork, and from what I see, there's nothing illegal going on."

Agent Breene stood and paced a few steps before continuing, then said, "Are you telling me you don't know much about the inner workings of the company?"

"That's correct. As a matter of fact, there are many things they don't include me in which has always surprised me."

"What do you mean surprised you - what kind of things?"

"For example, when the company bids on a new housing project, I'm not asked to provide any financial information for the submission."

Agent Breene scratched his neck, wrinkled his forehead, and began to look irritated. "That's unusual is it?"

"Yes, very unusual. When I worked for the CPA firm, I often did compilations and summaries for clients in the bidding process. When I took the job at Homeward, I naturally thought that would be an area I could add value having a great deal of experience. I was under the impression that was one reason Bobby hired me. I was wrong. I'm just a transaction man. It's honestly disappointing."

Agent Breene was frowning in silence. He too was clearly disappointed.

"Mr. Gable, we had hoped you were more entrenched in the organization. Seems we were wrong. Since you are not in the family, we had hoped you could help us. Your loyalty to the company wouldn't run as deep as a family member. They apparently have not entrusted you with much information. I wonder if you could change that. Help us get the information we need."

"I'm sure I don't know what you are getting at, but I need to get back to my family soon. Can we wrap this up?"

"Sure. Get back to your picnic. I have to give this some thought before proceeding." He then pulled a card from his pocket and handed it to William. "Here's my number. I'll be in touch but feel free to call me anytime. Specifically, if anything develops....say you overhear something that might be important or just doesn't feel right. Be on your toes now....and, be cautious. Don't say anything to anyone at work about our talk."

"I certainly won't. As a matter of fact, yesterday, the meeting I had to attend was with the owner, Bobby. He knows something's up and told me to defer to our lawyers if anyone asks me anything. I didn't say a word about my conversation with you before I went into work."

"Thank you, William, you did the right thing. We'll talk again."

The Agent then turned and walked away leaving William holding the card. A rush of feelings overcame him. Fear, uncertainty, confusion, you name it, he was feeling it. He paused for a few moments to gain some composure before returning to Suzanne and Ellie. He was determined this would not ruin their day.

The family spent the rest of the day at the park and enjoyed their picnic as planned. William managed to remain focused on the family, staying in the moment. When they returned home, after Ellie was laid in her bed for a nap, Suzanne questioned him about the meeting with Agent Breene.

"Now that we have some time alone, what did the FBI agent have to say at the Park?"

William chose to divulge minimal information, just answer her questions. "Not much, but it is about Homeward Enterprises. They *are* under investigation."

"For what?"

"He didn't say."

"You didn't ask?" She replied with irritation in her voice.

"No, I didn't. I just told him I didn't know anything and that I needed to get back to my family."

"But William, this was a chance for you to find out more about what's going on."

"He gave me his card and said to call him if I thought of anything that might help. I agree with what you said last night. It's better that I don't know much, and I should keep it that way. Hopefully, this will all blow over as Bobby said and nothing will come of it."

"I'm surprised he was satisfied with that. Didn't he try to get any information from you about the Company?"

"No, he said he had to think about it. He was disappointed when I told him they don't share much with me. If you think about it, just because the FBI is investigating Homeward doesn't mean they have done anything wrong. Maybe Bobby what right that one of his competitors has it out for him because he's the one doing a lot of business with the State."

That pretty much ended the conversation on the subject and William made a decision, he would tell her as little as possible going forward. He would handle this on his own because he could see it was starting to upset her. No need for her to worry. Maybe nothing much would come of it anyway, and as Bobby said, the lawyers would handle it.

Chapter Four

Sunday was another special day with family. William's mother, Eleanor, lived out in the country nearby and every Sunday she prepared a feast. She lived alone in early retirement after taking care of William's father for two years before he lost his battle with cancer. She had spent her working years as a high school business teacher, and now her first grandchild filled the emptiness in her life that came from the loss of her husband – the love of her life.

Eleanor was always a strong, no-nonsense woman. She raised William as a working mother, but nothing ever seemed to suffer. She took her duties as a wife, mother, and teacher with equal dedication and endless energy. William's admiration and love for his mother had developed over the years beginning in childhood and increased as he witnessed her response to life's challenges into his adulthood. He was happy to have brought so much joy to her life when he married Suzanne and then again when Ellie was born.

For Eleanor, every Sunday was more like a celebration. She spent much of the week getting ready with grocery shopping for the special meal that included a delicious dessert, and she couldn't resist adding a new toy to the toy chest or a new outfit for Ellie. She considered spoiling her granddaughter her right and mission in life. Luckily there was no one who dared stand in her way.

Even when Ellie was just a few months old, she didn't mind having her overnight so her son and daughter-in-law could spend some time alone. She turned one of the spare bedrooms into a nursery as soon as Ellie was born. Even if the baby came for just the afternoon or needed a nap on Sunday when the family came for dinner, she wanted Ellie to have a comfortable place of her own.

Eleanor was looking forward to each coming year as her granddaughter grew. She would change the furnishings and decor of the room to accommodate that growth. As a teacher, she loved stocking the room with books and also set up a little reading corner with an oversized chair they could both sit in together. Her love of books would be passed on to Ellie.

As much as she loved raising her son, the role of grandmother took on a higher level of joy and excitement that she found difficult to explain. One thing Eleanor knew for sure – she was glad they lived in the same area so that she would be involved in Ellie's life and develop a bond with her over the years.

At the same time, she knew it was important not to overstep her bounds. She trusted William and his wife to raise their daughter as they wished and Eleanor was careful about offering unsolicited advice. She was content to be involved as much as they needed and wanted, but no more and she had other interests of her own. She was busy with her women's bridge club, church choir, and involvement in the school where she had taught volunteering for functions to raise funds for the parent teachers' association.

She also had a lot of friends to do things with like shopping, wine tasting, and occasional trips to the casino for a little play on the slots. Her late husband would have wanted her to enjoy life, and she had no problem getting out and doing as much of that as she could.

Ellie was just over one year old, but Eleanor was looking forward to her second birthday. She was thinking about getting new things for her room, in preparation for potty training, feeding herself, and what fun the new books and toys would bring. She could hardly contain herself as each passing day brought more anticipation of the years to come. She was, however, happy to enjoy spending time with Ellie in her role as grandparent and balancing that with her personal interests.

Just as she was putting the finishing touches on the three-layer chocolate cake, Eleanor heard a car pull into the driveway. She rushed to the front door and smiled at the sight of William carrying Ellie up the steps.

"Hi, guys!"

"Hi, Mom. How are you?" he asked as he handed Ellie over to Eleanor. It was always the first thing he did when they arrived for Sunday dinner at Eleanor's insistence.

"Oh, I'm doing great and so happy you are here. I have a few surprises for Miss Ellie in her room."

"Why am I not surprised that you have a few surprises for her?"

Suzanne then chimed in, "Yes, Eleanor, we're not surprised. I'd be worried about you if you didn't. Now, is there anything I can do in the kitchen while you spend some time with Ellie?"

"Nope. Everything's all set. I was just adding some sprinkles to the chocolate cake when you pulled in, and everything else is under control."

"Sounds good, Mom. I think I'll get us some iced tea and we'll sit on the front porch for a while. Such a beautiful day and so nice to get out here where the air is fresh and clean away from the city." Eleanor proceeded to Ellie's room to play while William and Suzanne settled in the rocking chairs on the porch with their drinks.

"You know, Suz, this reminds me so much of my childhood, a day just like today, sitting here on the porch." He ended with his eyes shut and took a big slow breath through his nose.

"I imagine it would," she answered with a smile.

"And every time we come out here, I start thinking about making a change - you know buying a place closer to Mom."

"Well, we can always consider it, and you know if we want to have another child, a bigger house with a yard would be nice. Ellie definitely enjoys running around outside when we're here."

He turned to her and said with conviction, "we should start looking, you know, we should do it! I enjoyed growing up out here, and I want that for Ellie."

She shook her head in agreement, "I'm ready when you are, William."

They enjoyed a delicious meal followed by dessert then Ellie took a brief nap giving the adults a little time for uninterrupted conversation.

"So, William," Eleanor started, "How's work going?"

"Much of the same. You know, boring accounting work. We're still busy with new projects, but nothing I can't handle." He made no mention of the FBI or the meeting with Bobby.

"That's good, and I'm so glad you decided to leave public accounting. I remember those weeks during tax season when you couldn't make Sunday dinner. Remember, Suzanne, before Ellie was born we would meet for lunch and do some shopping?"

Suzanne replied shaking her head, "Yup, I remember. I hated those last few weeks, but you and I did enjoy our time together. I was very glad to have you around to help me get through it."

"Well, I was happy to take advantage of those days to get to know my daughter-in-law a little better."

With a smile, Suzanne replied, "me too."

"I have an idea for the holidays this year. I was thinking of doing an old fashioned Christmas here at the house. Maybe the three of you could pack up and come out for a few days. I'll get one of the rooms ready for you two and Ellie, of course, will sleep in her room. We can keep a fire burning in the fireplace, even cut a tree from the property and decorate it together. What do you think?"

William at first looked at Suzanne not wanting to answer quickly. It was, after all, a time he knew she'd enjoy with Ellie at their house.

Sensing this hesitation, Eleanor continued, "I'm sorry I should've realized you two want to spend Christmas in your home. Maybe we could do it on a weekend before or after Christmas."

Suzanne was the next to speak, "No, honestly, if it's alright with William, I think that would be fantastic, like an extended Sunday dinner. Maybe William and I could take a couple of walks on the property….alone…while you have some time with Ellie. What do you think, William?"

"I'm totally fine with it, just as long as you are."

"Well only if you're both sure," Eleanor said with a little smile trying to contain her excitement

"Hey, I spent a lot of Christmases here and loved every one of them. And you know what, Mom? I think it would be nice for you to not be alone here in this big house. Just promise me one thing."

"What's that? And don't tell me I can't have a mountain of gifts for my granddaughter under the tree, I won't agree to that stipulation."

"Don't worry. I know better than that! But seriously, I don't want you working like one of old man Simmons' workhorses and tiring yourself out. You have to let us help, okay?" he emphasized those last words looking her straight in the eyes.

"Alright, I hear ya. I can agree to that. We will *work and play with equal vigor* - as your dad used to say."

Eleanor knew she would enjoy the weeks leading up to the holidays as she planned and prepared for having her little family at the house. They may be able to pitch in while there, but no one could control her before the time arrived, and she was going to go all out this year.

Suzanne's response to the idea of spending the holiday with Eleanor was predictable. She had no family of her own outside of William and Ellie and very little fond memories of holiday traditions. She had grown up in foster care, the child of alcoholic parents who lost her due to neglect. Her relationship with Eleanor was one she cherished because, for once in her life, she felt the love from a parent as she had never experienced before. Suzanne thought of Eleanor as the mother she never had and holidays, since meeting William, were joyful. She would look forward to spending this Christmas with her family including Eleanor.

Later as the family headed for home, Eleanor waved from the front porch. As she watched them drive away, a strange sensation crept into her body. It wasn't the first time she felt this way, a sort of intuition that something was stirring. She always knew, whether good or bad, when something was coming. This time it wasn't a good feeling. She shuddered a bit then shook it off, turned and entered the house thinking, *you're an old fool, Eleanor. All is right with the world.*

Chapter Five

Monday morning, boy the weekends go by too fast, William thought as he pulled into his office parking garage with a certain level of dread. He was worried he would see Agent Breene but was pleasantly surprised. No incident. He entered his office as routinely as any other Monday.

He began his day by looking through invoices that needed to be paid and checked the bank account balances online to make sure they had enough cash to cover. If not, he would transfer funds from the higher interest money market account. He was a little short and needed just a few thousand and accessed the account to prepare a transfer.

William didn't pay much attention to the money market account, or any one of several other investment accounts the business maintained because Bobby had instructed him to focus on the checking account. He said William's responsibility was to pay the bills and he would always make sure there would never be a cash flow problem.

William fully intended to work in his usual way, sticking to his routine, but Agent Breene's words kept entering his thoughts, 'I wonder if you could change that. Help us get the information we need.'

William paused after making the funds transfer to cover the invoices and thought, *is there anything here for me to find? Could there be any transactions that would uncover illegal practices? Is there something right under my nose that I didn't see before merely because I wasn't looking?*

He began to stop thinking like an accountant and stepped back into the role of auditor deciding to approach this from a different perspective. He would perform a financial audit as if the Company was a client and he was hired to audit the books. He would assume they wanted assurance that the financial reporting was accurate and that no fraudulent transactions existed, no embezzlement, employee collusion, or suspicious activity was present.

He didn't think there was anything to find and after performing the audit, he could show Agent Breene this was a dead end, and they would have to leave him and Homeward alone. He hoped to end the FBI investigation, and Bobby would never even need to know about William's involvement.

Since William was the only person recording transactions through the operating checking account, he felt confident there would be nothing of interest there. He reviewed the transactions regularly and performed a monthly reconciliation to the bank. If anything hit that account that he didn't record himself, he would be aware of it.

He started by making a checklist of things he would look for in the other accounts beginning with the money market account. This checklist was something he was familiar with having planned many financial audits in the past.

Cash transactions were a good place to start when looking for illegal activity. Things like unusually large deposits or withdrawals, purchases of cashier's checks, transfers between accounts, and an increase in the number or size of cash transactions.

He would also look for any patterns. Some examples included multiple transactions in the same amount or at consistent intervals of time. Then he would compare tax returns, for both corporate and payroll taxes, to the revenue and profit figures reported in the financial statements verifying consistency. He would prepare and review cash flow statements and look for any excessive amounts of cash either coming in or going out not substantiated by profit levels.

Homeward was a privately held company meaning they did not offer stock sales traded on the open market. Therefore, they were not required to have an annual external audit performed by a CPA, but because they received state grants and other funding, they were required to file information returns and reports. He could review those against internal financial reports to see if anything didn't jive. He didn't suspect he would find any discrepancies here, but if Bobby was involved in something dirty, the audit would help William uncover it.

As he mapped out his audit plan, he began to feel his adrenalin rise. This might be a good way to make his boring job a little more interesting. He decided over the next couple of weeks he would work through the plan and organize the information he collected, being careful to lock things up in his desk or bring copies of documents and notes home to make sure Bobby didn't stumble on what he was doing. He also decided not to put anything related to his audit on his computer. He would have to write things on his legal pad and transcribe later at home.

"Agent Breene? This is William Gable," he announced when the man answered the phone.

"Yes, William. Good to hear from you."

"It's been a couple of weeks since we met at the park and you said to call if there was anything I thought I could help you with."

"Did you find anything you think is important that we should discuss?" The Agent sounded cautiously hopeful.

He knew from experience, getting evidence to convict in white collar crimes was a rarity. After his meeting with William in the park, he wasn't sure Homeward's accountant was going to be worthy of pursuit as an informant.

"Yes, I think I may be onto something. I've been looking into the bank accounts, and I'm seeing unusual transactions and some patterns that I can't yet substantiate."

The Agent answered with a lift in his voice, "Good. I'd like to know what you've found, we should meet."

He suggested an out-of-the-way diner and agreed to meet the following Saturday morning for breakfast. When William arrived, he noticed Agent Breene lost his suit, hat, and overcoat, now dressed in jeans, a polo shirt, and sweater. They sat in a booth towards the back and shared a meal as they talked.

William began by explaining his approach, how he had decided to perform a financial audit. After he finished going through his audit plan, Agent Breene asked, "What types of things did you find?"

"Mostly odd things related to cash, things that would prompt the auditor to expand the scope of the audit, in other words, the need for more digging."

William then reached into his backpack for a file. He had decided he should use a backpack instead of his briefcase making it look more casual. Then he continued as he went through some of the papers in the file.

"I've been taking notes, first with a list of the audit tests I performed and then of the unusual transactions I found. I also have copies of bank statements, invoices, and anything else related to that list."

Agent Breene looked on with interest saying, "Exactly what did you find?"

"Well, here's the list. In the money market account, I found several cash deposits all in even dollar amounts in multiples of $1,000." His list included dates with corresponding amounts of $1,000, $2,000, all the way up to $10,000 each. Then he continued, "I was able to trace the dates back to the completion of specific building projects, all of which are those we built for the State. Then I found some patterns with the subcontractors we use for those units. For example, we've been using a small group of subcontractors for foundation, sprinkler systems, and paving consistently on those projects. The odd thing is we don't use that same group when we build our own complexes that have nothing to do with the State."

"What do you mean when they have nothing to do with the State?" Agent Breene asked.

"We have some complexes we build that are exclusively owned, financed, and run by Homeward. We receive no grants, loans or breaks from the State. On those, we use a lot of different subcontractors or our own workers, and I don't see any pattern there. The rent we charge for those apartments is market-based and highly profitable."

"Are you involved in any way deciding who gets the subcontract work on any projects?"

"No, not at all. I don't even see the bids. What I get from Bobby on each project is a folder with a cover sheet that gives details about the job including who is subcontracted to do what. As the work is completed, the subcontractors invoice us, and I pay them."

"Seems a little unusual. Anything else?"

"Another odd thing I found is with the payments for work. The subcontractor payments are considerably higher on jobs that we do for the State, as I said before, where the state owns the building or where the units are subsidized with respect to rent. On the other hand, when Homeward owns the building with no State assistance in funding, we pay a lot less for the subcontract work."

He then went over a spreadsheet he had prepared comparing amounts paid to subcontractors on State jobs and those exclusive to Homeward projects.

Agent Breene smiled and said, "Now William, I think you're on to something. This is some great work you've done. Are you are willing to continue?"

"Yes, I'm willing if you think Bobby's up to something illegal and what I'm able to provide is relevant. I've had some second thoughts because he's been good to me, but if his illegal activity is the basis for his generosity, I can't continue to benefit from that with a clear conscience."

Agent Breene nodded and said, "believe me, William, Bobby's involved in something, not sure exactly what yet, but with what you've told me and shown me today, I'm sure we at least have a starting point, something to go on."

Agent Breene then spent the rest of the meeting giving William some tips on how to proceed with his work. He explained that William would need to work like a forensic accountant, sort of an extension of a financial auditor. He would no longer be looking for misrepresentations within the financial statements of a business, he would now be looking to identify irregularities that would uncover and provide evidence of a crime to be used in a criminal case against Bobby.

William continued to dig into his company's records, making notes and collecting copies of related documents. He became comfortable with the Agent, a feeling he had never experienced with Bobby. He also did some research at home in the evening looking into the field of forensic accounting and found his research easy to understand given his background. He found it interesting, even exhilarating. For the first time since joining Homeward, he was genuinely enjoying his work.

The two men met at the diner on a regular basis, but as time went on William started to wonder if they were getting anywhere on the investigation. He must have been providing useful information, or the Agent wouldn't continue the relationship, but their conversations were pretty much one-sided. Agent Breene asked all the questions while William answered and then divulged lists of the documents he was able to accumulate. His curiosity was growing, and he wanted to know where they stood.

"Agent Breene? I wondered if you could answer a question for me."

"Sure, William. If I can, I will."

"I've been copying financial records that I think might help and have kept a log of bids, contracts, and meetings, but you've never said what you suspect Bobby of being involved in. What illegal activity do you think he's into?"

Agent Breene paused in thought for a moment. He looked as if he was considering options as to how to proceed, then he answered cautiously, "Okay, I'll answer your question, and I know I don't have to tell you this is highly confidential. You, William, have become an informant and with that comes a degree of trust between us. Information that I share with you cannot be told to anyone....not even Suzanne. Understand?"

"Yes, of course, I understand. I haven't been telling her anything since our second meeting. It seems like this is something she would just worry about and I consider it something I have to do on my own."

"Very good. Now, to answer your question. We suspect Bobby's involved in several illegal activities such as bid rigging, price fixing, and other forms of collusion. Along with these types of activities we usually find bribery as well. Remember the transactions that you discovered with the deposits of cash to the money market account?"

"Yes, the ones that made me start to keep a file for you. I remember. Was that significant?"

"It was," Agent Breene answered. "Very significant because it's a sign Bobby could be linked to corruption in the State Department of Housing and Development. We've wondered how one company could be awarded so many state contracts to build low-income housing and more importantly, how could they be expanding across the entire state so rapidly."

"What lead you to Bobby and his company?"

"This appeared on our radar when someone sent an anonymous letter to the bureau complaining about Bobby's winning one particular contract. It was the first contract he secured in that county, and we believe the tip must have come from a competitor. At first, we thought it was sour grapes, but we take every tip seriously, and our research initially showed Bobby's company could be favored in contract awards and in funding from various State agencies to build and maintain his properties."

"But why would anyone pay Bobby? Wouldn't it make more sense for Bobby to pay someone in the government to get the contract?"

"If Bobby's the top man, there are any number of players that pay him to get in on the scheme - suppliers, subcontractors, and inspectors to name a few."

"Alright, explain this bid rigging to me. How does it work?"

"Usually it involves a group of competitors, such as contractors like Bobby bidding on the same housing projects. It can take many forms. Bid suppression is one where the competitors agree to not bid on a project so that one wins. Then there's complementary bidding where some bids will be much higher or require terms and conditions that are unreasonable, paving the way for one specific bidder."

William was listening intently but was still confused.

"I'm starting to understand how it's done and that there're different ways of doing it, but I still don't see why. What does anyone get out of it?"

"Eliminating competition, paving the way for everyone in the group to capitalize on contracts paid with government funds, which ultimately are supported by taxpayer dollars. The competitors conspire to inflate prices from purchasers that solicit competitive bids, for example, state and local governments. And subcontracting is an offshoot of bid rigging."

"Sounds like a lot of people could be involved."

"Right. It's like this. The company getting the contract agrees to subcontract parts of the project out to the other bidders involved in the scheme. The bids aren't as low as they would be if they were under true competition. The group may also take some losses on a few projects, in the beginning, to keep the bids low and squeeze out those that aren't willing to get involved in the scheme. Once the group involved in the collusion is established, higher bids can be submitted, and government funds can flow throughout the group. Then cash goes back into the hands of the individuals in government offices in the form of bribes, those making sure the bids go to the right company."

"Oh, wow, so the one complaint you received may have come from someone who wasn't in the group. Maybe even a company that the group tried to bring in and couldn't because they chose to do things legally."

"That's right, William, you're getting it. The thing is, we don't know who's involved, but we think we're going to find this runs deep and there are many players. What we need to understand is who's facilitating this from inside. Who is Bobby connected with within the State helping his group secure these contracts."

"I have to believe those cash payments to Bobby must be coming from those benefitting from Bobby's State contracts. Now, if I could just find out if he is paying bribes and to whom...." William paused, deep in thought, his wheels obviously turning.

"William, I think you're going to be more help to us than I originally thought. I've seen that look before."

"What look?" William asked.

Agent Breene smiled and shook his head as he continued, "That look that says you've reached the point of no return. You're hooked, one of the good guys and putting away the bad guys is exciting."

William replied, "I have to admit, I do find it exhilarating. I've always appreciated the job, but don't like illegal activity, and no matter how much I like Bobby and my work, nothing is worth getting involved in that. I want to be on the right side."

"Exactly, but not everyone is willing to do what you're doing, and we need people like you to help us. You were just in the right place at the right time, and we're fortunate that you're not involved in the corruption."

William moved in closer wanting to keep his voice low as he asked, "So how exactly do the multiple deposits of cash lead you to believe he's taking bribes?"

"In this case, they may just be kickbacks." The agent went on to explain. "Since you were able to connect the deposits to dates related to projects with the State, we believe Bobby is running a bid rigging scheme with a group of contractors and subcontractors. The group agrees on a plan to submit bids. They make sure one contractor, usually Bobby, secures the project and they probably know ahead of time how the subcontract work will be designated and how much each participant will be paid.

They also decide how much each will kick back to Bobby and that's where the cash deposits come into play. If someone in the housing department is involved in helping Bobby's group get contracts and funding, the group will also slip cash to them in the form of a bribe."

William was getting the picture but then wondered about something else, so he asked, "There's something that's always puzzled me though. Why did Bobby hire me? You'd think he would want to have only people connected to the family especially in the finance position."

Agent Breene then explained his take on it, "I think the reason people like Bobby, hire people like you is this - they hope it helps them appear above board. Looking at the timeline, it seems he may have hired you when he began to feel he was under suspicion. There may have even been a plan to feel you out and at some point bring you into the game, but early on he must have realized you were not someone he could trust with the truth. You couldn't be turned to illegal activity. That's why, as you said, he didn't involve you in many of their business dealings. You became just a highly compensated bookkeeper. "

"Do you think Bobby suspects me in any way?"

"No not at this point. You would have seen signs, but the deeper we go, the higher the risk so you have to be careful. So always maintain as much normalcy in your behavior. Bobby's not stupid, and he will be on his guard."

"Here's another question. Why does someone in the government want to award Bobby so many contracts? What do they get out of it besides a little cash?"

Agent Breene smiled and said, "That, my friend is something we don't know yet. If we knew the answer to that question, we would be closer to finding out who's involved. It could be something as simple as greed, a way to get taxpayer dollars to those who will pay bribes to get the business. For example, Bobby could have a connection to someone working in the office that awards contracts and the two of them work together to form a bid rigging group. Bobby and the subcontractors get a majority of the business and then pay off their man inside."

"So you think those cash deposits are coming from subcontractors?"

"We aren't sure. We assume from the subcontractors, but we don't know if they're all involved. We're using the dates and names to investigate further, looking for evidence of collusion."

William wasn't totally satisfied. "I understand greed, but could it be more than that, more than just bribes to get government funds and increase business?"

"Sure. Anything's possible. We won't know until the evidence leads us to the truth. This could be a small time bid rigging scheme with Bobby at the top leading a group of subcontractors with everyone getting rich off taxpayer funds with a contact or two in the housing department. Or Bobby and his people could be a small part of a bigger ring of corruption. Time will tell, William, time will tell."

Chapter Six

It's been said when you stand up for what's right, be prepared to stand alone. William felt alone. It was Monday morning, and he was trying to work, but couldn't stop his distracted thoughts of the events of the past few months. He knew he was doing the right thing helping the FBI and the evidence he was collecting was mounting. He wasn't sure what it all meant, but he knew it was going to help put Bobby away. That, however, was the minor score. Any state government officials, if involved, would be the bigger prize.

With Agent Breene instructing him on investigative methods, William found ways to look deeper inside Bobby's business. He listened in on conversations, reviewed Bobby's calendar and dug through his office at night when working alone late in the evening. Bobby was sloppy and usually left his computer unlocked during working hours giving William the opportunity to peruse when Bobby left the office for lunch. There were a few close calls, but in the end, Bobby thought William was still his hardworking bookkeeper none the wiser. Sometimes William thought, *Bobby must think I'm an idiot!*

William was a very smart man, and his work in forensic accounting on this case proved that. His thoughts of a future in that field were developing as he realized lately that he would not be working for Bobby much longer. At some point, the FBI would crack this case wide open, Bobby would be arrested along with all family members involved, and William would be looking for a new job.

He had to admit, he enjoyed what he'd been doing for the FBI, and with his background as a CPA, he could certainly make a move to the more specialized field of forensic accounting. It would require additional education, but he was willing to pick up additional graduate courses once this part of his life was put behind him.

The phone rang, he jumped a little, picked up the receiver and said, "William Gable."

"Billy. It's Bobby."

"Oh, hi Bobby. What's up?"

"I need ya to meet me. We gotta talk."

"Sure, Bobby. Are you in yet?"

"No. We can't talk there. Come to Lou's Grill, ya know the one my cousin owns. We had my wife's birthday party there last year." And he hung up.

William was going to ask why they couldn't meet in the office, and he was about to say *Now?* But he didn't get the chance. He grabbed his coat and headed out the door to meet Bobby.

Then it hit him, and he thought, *Is it safe? Is Bobby on to me?* He took his cellphone out of his pocket and called Agent Breene to let him know where he was going. Agent Breene calmed him down and said he would send someone there to keep an eye on things. He also told him to keep it casual and listen to what Bobby had to say. The case against him was tightening up and would be out in the open soon. *Hold on* he told William, *we are almost there.*

When William entered the restaurant, he noticed it was pretty crowded which made him feel better. He had envisioned it empty with a closed sign on the door and just Bobby sitting at a table with a couple of goons standing at each side. He wondered if anyone at a table or booth was an FBI agent, he sure hoped so.

"Billy, thanks for comin'. Sit down. What'll ya have?" Bobby said as William approached the table.

"Hey, Bobby. Sure thanks. I didn't get breakfast today, so I'll have eggs over easy, toast and bacon."

William thought if he ordered breakfast, he would appear relaxed and comfortable. Inside he was a mess, and he could feel sweat dribbling down his back.

Bobby waved the server over and repeated William's order adding some coffee with a shot of whiskey. Then he winked at William and said, "You're gonna need it, trust me."

"What's going on, Bobby?"

"There's somethin' I gotta tell you because, well, you're my numbers guy, and I want to make sure you understand where your loyalties are, ya know?"

"No, not really," William answered as calmly as he could.

"See it's like this. We do a lot of work across the state building housing units with some government funds. Well, some people get the idea we're involved in some kind of scam with bribes and kickbacks and what not."

"You're not doing any of that, right?"

"Of course not. I mean I have some connections, and one hand washes tha other, but it's just the way business is done. So here's tha thing. You remember we talked before about the company being under some suspicion and that our lawyers were handling everything, right?"

"Yes, Bobby, I remember. I thought it came to nothing."

"You're right, but I'm thinking you might get asked about what goes on in our business and if you have any information, maybe even be asked to testify if they ever try to pin anything on me, so I wanted to take you into my confidence on a few things."

"What things?" William asked.

"You've been working for me a long time now, what like four years?"

"That's about right."

"I think it's time you get more involved and help with the growth of our business, learn more about how we operate. And there's more money and perks that go along with that too. I want you to be more involved so you can vouch for me and my business. You know we do things right so I expect you to have my back."

"Oh, I don't know, Bobby," William replied. "I'm satisfied with my work and compensation now and with a young family, maybe ready to have another child soon. I don't know if I want more responsibility."

"Sure, the family, I understand family, and you do have..... a beautiful family, Billy."

William didn't like the way he said that last part. Maybe he was just paranoid, but it sounded a little bit too much like a reminder in a threatening way.

Bobby continued, "Let's put our cards on the table. You work for me, and I've done right by you. Now it's time to take the next step and come into the family, my family. I want you to go along with Mitch and see more of our operation, learn more, get more involved. I gotta ask for your loyalty. If we're ever falsely accused, and I mean falsely, as my numbers guy, I'll count on you to do right by me."

At this point William became uneasy with the direction the conversation was taking, but then he realized this was a way for him to help the FBI. If they are getting close anyway and it would be over soon, why not play along and see where it goes.

"Okay, Bobby, I see what you mean. I can get more involved, and if you think I should work with Mitch, I'm willing to do that."

They finished their breakfast and William returned to his office. He figured the FBI may have had someone close by to listen in, but he would wait for Agent Breene to contact him and hopefully meet soon to discuss his next step.

After work, he went to the gym. He needed to de-stress after his meeting with Bobby. It seemed like a shift in direction, and he didn't want Suzanne to sense his mood. He liked a good steam after his workout, and when he entered the steam room, he found just one man with a towel over his head sitting on the bench. After sitting down, the man removed his towel and William was surprised to see Agent Breene emerge from underneath.

"Oh, geez, you startled me."

"Sorry, William. This was the only way. Things have changed. We have your conversation at breakfast recorded. Our man was in a booth near your table. Smart thing calling me to give me the meeting place. You may have been compromised, but we're not sure."

William replied with concern, "What do you mean compromised?"

"This turn of events could be one of two things. Either Bobby suspects you have already been approached by us or he knows it's only a matter of time."

"Which do you think it is?"

"We're almost certain it's the latter, and he's setting you up so that if we do ask for your help, you'll already be involved and he can convince you of your impending guilt along with him."

"MY guilt? How could I be guilty in his scheme?"

"You may learn first-hand the extent of the illegal activity, and if you know about it, you can be considered an accomplice."

With concern, William asked, "Is that true or is that just what Bobby might believe to be true?"

"If you work for Bobby and he's involved in illegal activity that you know about, yes, you can be considered an accomplice, but since you're working with us as an informant, you are not guilty of any crimes. The beauty is, Bobby doesn't know that."

"I hope you're right. What now?"

"You have a decision to make. You can stop now, and we will take what you have given us so far, or you can go in deeper and get us more."

"What if you're wrong and he is on to me?"

"I'm not going to lie to you. That could mean trouble for you."

"You mean he could hurt me or someone in my family?"

"I wouldn't put it past him. I know he's been good to you, but don't let that fool you, William."

"Why? Is there something you're not telling me?"

"You know Bobby's cousin, his former bookkeeper?"

"Yeah, the one that retired and moved to Florida."

"We're not sure that's what happened. We can't find him."

"Oh, shit!" William exclaimed, "you think something bad happened to him?"

"We just don't know, but can't rule it out unless we find him. I will tell you there are things we can put into place to protect you and your family as much as possible, but the deeper you go, the more he confides in you, the higher the risk."

Without hesitation, William answered, "I'll do it. Set me up, tell me what to do, and just do one more thing for me."

"What's that?"

"Make sure you protect my family. My wife, daughter, and my mother need protection. I'm sure you heard his comment about my family. Was I wrong in sensing something in that?"

"No, William, you weren't wrong, and I have to warn you, he'll keep using your devotion to your family against you to tighten his grip. Be prepared."

"Can you assure me you'll be able to protect them?"

"We'll do all in our power, but unfortunately it's part of the risk. Now, are you still willing to keep this going?"

"I'm all in as far as I'm concerned, but I feel it's only fair to Suzanne to fill her in as appropriate and make sure she supports me in this."

"I understand. Let her know you are assisting with this investigation, but you can't give her any details."

"Okay, Agent Breene, I'll talk to Suzanne and get back to you."

"You may want to let your mother know as well. Then make your final decision and we'll talk. We can alert them to any precautions they should take."

"Okay," William replied, "I'll be in touch as soon as I can."

Chapter Seven

That following weekend William asked Eleanor to come to dinner. After dessert was finished and Ellie was put to bed, he poured everyone a glass of wine and said he had something important to discuss with them.

"I need to talk to you both about something that's come up at work, and it involves us all. Suzanne, you won't be surprised by this, but Mom this is something I haven't told you about so here goes.

I've been working with the FBI on an investigation that involves my boss, Bobby, and his business dealings. It seems there's some illegal activity with his government contracts and funding sources. I can't give you any more details, but Bobby wants me to get more involved in the business, and if I do that, I can probably get more information for the FBI."

He decided to pause and let it sink in a little before he continued. Suzanne was the first to respond.

"You mean this has been going on since the FBI approached you months ago?"

"Yes, that's right. I didn't tell you anything after that because I didn't want you to worry and I'm not supposed to discuss this with anyone."

Suzanne became silent.

"Then why now?" Eleanor asked.

"Things have changed. At first, I was just doing what I could to find things out around the office, but now Bobby wants to take me into his confidence and have me learn more about his business. The FBI agent thinks I can go deeper now and learn more. The thing is, it's also riskier, and I've asked for both of you and Ellie to be provided protection."

"William, I know what kind of man you are." Eleanor began, "and I'm sure you want to do all you can to help, but you do have a family now."

"I know you're right," William replied. "And I realize it's putting us all in danger. That's why I wanted to talk to both of you about it."

"Your family depends on you. Are you sure you want to put all this at risk?" Eleanor asked with concern in her voice.

"No, I'm not sure, that's why I want to know what you both think." They all sat quietly for several minutes. Eleanor was carefully considering her response.

"Honestly, William, Suzanne, I think this is something the two of you should talk about in private and decide. I know it affects me, but so much less than the two of you. I'll support whatever decision you make, and so now I'll be on my way and leave you to it."

"I see your point, Mom, but don't you want to say one way or the other what you think I should do?" William asked not wanting let her feel she didn't have a say.

"I've said enough. Don't worry about any risk on my part, I'll buck up and keep my guard up. Just keep me informed." With that, she gave them both a hug and headed out the door.

Suzanne sat quietly on the sofa for several minutes. She was at a loss for words, and then she stood up and started to leave the room. Suddenly, she turned and looked at William with eyes on fire. He realized her silence while Eleanor was there was due to a growing anger inside.

"Why have you kept this from me all this time? You said you thought it would turn out to be nothing, and now you tell me you've been working with the FBI. I'm stunned!" She stood in front of him, her voice rising louder with each word.

"I know I'm sorry. I didn't want to worry you. You seemed to get upset after my second meeting with Agent Breene, and I made the decision to go it alone."

"William! We don't do things that way. We don't keep things from each other. Why? Why now?"

"First, let's sit down. I know you're mad, but we have to talk about it calmly. This is important."

"You're damn right it's important. But apparently you didn't think it was important enough until now to let me in on it. And I'm sorry. I'm not ready to sit down." She paced the floor and William continued.

"Suz, listen, I know we always share with each other, and we've always supported each other, but this whole situation is slightly different. There was a point where Agent Breene instructed me not to tell anyone. Please, try to understand. I have been put in a very difficult position."

With tears starting to well in her eyes, she said, "I don't care what kind of position you found yourself in, we have never lied to each other, and I want to know why."

William came to face her. He placed both hands on her shoulders looking into her eyes choosing not to speak for a moment. He brought a thumb slowly to one eye then the other and wiped away her tears. She softened slightly, but he could tell she was still upset. When he felt she was beginning to calm down, he helped her to the sofa, and they both sat down.

With a sigh, she said, "You're right we have to talk about this. I'm sorry I started yelling. I guess I felt blindsided. Truthfully, I'm a little surprised I didn't sense more was going on. I thought I knew you so well."

"I've been trying to keep it to myself, but I can't do that any longer. Agent Breene wants my decision soon after talking with you and my mother. He said because of the risk you two need some protection, and he would work with us all, so we understand what's involved."

"Do you have a choice?" she asked, hopeful.

"Yes, I do. He said they can take all I have done to this point and I can stop, walk away and not accept Bobby's offer to get more involved in the business. I suppose I could just quit if he didn't like my refusal. Then I would look for another position, and the FBI would use my work as evidence in building their case along with everything else they have. I'm sure they have more than what I've given them."

He was willing to give it all up if she wanted him to. At one point, Suzanne pointed out to him the fact that he had already been gathering information for the FBI and Bobby would, at the very least, assume that if he was ever arrested.

They continued to discuss all that had happened and tried to agree on what to do, but Suzanne was clearly undecided.

"Listen, William, I know you have to give Agent Breene your answer, but I need some time to think. I'm glad you have a choice in the matter, and if it were just you and me to consider, I would right here and now say, forge ahead. The reality is we have a daughter, have you thought of that?" Her voice escalated as she reached the end of her comment.

"Yes, of course, I have. Hell, I've been thinking about her every step of the way, and of you. I don't want to put anyone in my family in harm's way. You know that, right? You know me?"

Before answering, she tossed her head back, looking up at the ceiling, and then said, "I do, but keeping this from me for all this time and then springing it on me, well it was surprising, and I'm trying to process it. My first thought is to walk away, but is that the right thing to do? I just don't know. I need time to think."

"I understand," he said and patted her leg gently. "I'll contact Agent Breene and ask him to give us a few more days."

Chapter Eight

Suzanne returned to the kitchen to clean up the breakfast dishes. With William at work and Ellie down for her morning nap, she had some time to think. Her intention was to get a little work done and then relax with a cup of tea. She knew she needed to give William an answer soon.

The one thing she realized after the discussion last night was that she was fortunate to have a husband who valued her opinion. She felt she had a say in this decision, a decision they would reach together. It was clear Eleanor would support their decision either way. Now she needed to decide what input she wanted to give William. Did she think he should continue to work with the FBI, or did she hope he would stop now, give them what he had, and be done with it? If he stopped, he could minimize the risk to himself and the family.

After loading the dishwasher, she turned and leaned on the sink, then slowly slid down to the floor. The tears began gradually, then flowed like running water and she did nothing to stop them. At the end of her crying jag, she found herself lying on the floor.

She had been trying to keep negative thoughts from invading her mind, never being one to back down from a challenge, but this time she felt disheartened. Her expectations were not extremely high for her life. All she ever wanted was what she now had, a loving husband, a child – eventually more children, and enough money to enjoy life in a modest way. That was it, and she didn't feel it was too much to ask for, yet now she felt there was some level of danger in losing it.

To her disappointment, in a way, she felt William's actions were, in part, responsible for that danger. It made her feel slightly naïve, and she asked herself, *how could I be so foolish to believe my life from the time I married William, would always be perfect? No one has that. The years of my childhood were not good – no family of my own – no stable home. My life with William has been like paradise in comparison. I finally have the family I've always wanted, but our future is full of uncertainty.*

As she rose to a sitting position, little by little, her feelings of anguish were replaced with relief then resolve. The tears she shed seemed to wash away some of what was pent up inside.

She wiped her face on a dish towel, took a deep breath and said aloud, "Come on girl. Now that that is over, get on with it. Time to think this through."

Fortunately, Ellie took a long nap and Suzanne spent the next hour in the den with a pot of tea and a journal. She jotted down some thoughts including the typical pros and cons list. Mostly there were cons, but she kept coming back to one thought that seemed to be driving her to a decision. She felt in her gut she knew what she wanted to tell William, but her mind kept her struggling with hesitation. Her thoughts were interrupted as the front doorbell rang. It was Eleanor.

"Eleanor, come in," she said with a smile. She was happy to see her mother-in-law and welcomed the interruption.

"I'm sorry to drop in like this without calling first," Eleanor said as she offered Suzanne a warm hug.

"Oh, please. It's fine. Ellie is down for a nap, and I was just having some tea. Would you like some?"

"I'd love some if you have a few minutes to talk that is." Eleanor headed for the den while Suzanne got another mug from the kitchen.

Once settled, Eleanor began, "Suzanne, this is not usually something I do, you know drop by unannounced, but I was on my way home from the craft store and had a strong feeling I should stop. I thought maybe you would like to talk about yesterday. If not, just say so, and we'll just have a normal visit."

"I'm glad you came. I've been struggling with this decision, and I could use some advice. Look, I made a pros and cons list. Seems silly, but I thought it would help."

"Did it?"

"No, not at all. The con side is full, and you'd think that would make this easy for me, as simple as that, right? But, here I sit going back and forth or in circles, I just do not know! What should I do?"

Eleanor paused in thought. She wanted to tell Suzanne what she thought she should do, what Eleanor herself would do if she were in Suzanne's place. But that wouldn't be right. This was Suzanne's decision.

Eleanor began slowly, "I wish I could tell you what to do, but I can't. This is something you and William have to work through. It'll affect the rest of your lives....and Ellie's. What I can do is listen, and as you talk through it, maybe together we can understand how you feel deep down about this situation. Then you can come to the decision you're comfortable with.

I've learned over the course of a lifetime that when we have a choice to make, we have to recognize that each choice comes with consequences. It's important that you think about how you'll feel about the choice you make. Will you be able to live with that decision?"

They spent the next couple of hours talking, even as Ellie got up from her nap and played quietly on the floor of the den. The conversation ended with Suzanne telling Eleanor she knew what to tell William. She also admitted it was just the decision she was driven to before Eleanor arrived that day, but now with Eleanor's help, she felt comfortable with that decision. Suzanne knew it was the only way, confident William would agree.

Later that evening with Ellie snug in her bed, Suzanne and William settled down in the living room with a bottle of wine. Suzanne began the conversation as she said, "I wanted to talk to you about the FBI investigation."

"Okay, shoot."

"I've given this a lot of thought, and even though I don't expect you to make your decision based solely on what I have to say, I want you to know I'm glad I have a say in this. Now, remember when you told me about the file you started shortly after you first talked to Agent Breene?"

William answered, "Yes, I remember and I know now I should have told you about it right then. Now I'm already in pretty deep and ..."

She chose not to let him continue, interrupting by saying, "That's what I'm getting at. I think you made your decision to help when you copied that first piece of paper. I understand it could get more dangerous, but you're already involved. It's already dangerous, we are already at risk."

With a sigh, he replied, "Yes, good point. I guess I didn't think about it like that. Now I realize I chose to do this, I was never pressured, and there were times I enjoyed it. Forensic accounting may be a career move for me."

She took his hands in hers, "Why stop now? It's the right thing to do, and we will be cautious and follow the FBI instructions."

He looked confused. "I don't get it. You were so mad about the whole thing when I told you I could continue or walk away. What changed?"

She said, "Time to think, basically. Remember, you've been going through this over time. I was in the dark thinking life was moving along as usual and making plans for another baby. I truly believed it had blown over as you said it would. Once I realized I couldn't just jump back into that protected little world, I moved on and made my decision on what I wanted to tell you. The one thing I know in my heart - you are not the kind of man that walks away when you're faced with doing what's right. You have ample cause to walk away given the safety of your family, but I think if you stopped now, it would haunt you."

"I know you're right. That's how I feel about it too, but I had to make sure you were in agreement because we could be in for a rough time of it."

"Well, let's just hope it doesn't go on too long and we can get back to our calm, happy life. Guess we better hold off on having another child for the time being."

William hugged her and whispered in her ear, "I'm so lucky to have you."

"And I'm lucky to have you - and Eleanor. She stopped by today, and we had a long talk. She didn't tell me what to do, but she helped me sort through my feelings about all this, and I was able to come to this decision with confidence."

"Oh, I see. Yes, my mother can be a good sounding board. I'm glad she was here for you today. We're both lucky to have her in our lives."

They agreed William would let Agent Breene know of his decision and ask that someone from the FBI meet with Suzanne and Eleanor to fill them in on any precautions they should take, what protection would be provided, and answer any questions they had.

That evening, Eleanor busied herself in Ellie's room. She had done some shopping the week before for some extra pajamas and clothes to keep at her house for when Ellie came to spend the night. With the new things washed and dried, she sat in the rocking chair folding and thinking. Her talk with Suzanne today was good for Suzanne, but Eleanor was conflicted.

Was I right to hold back on conveying my true feelings about the situation that entwined William and Suzanne? I don't even know what Suzanne has decided. Should I have asked her and then offered my thoughts? No, I'm sure I did the right thing. Now, I have to be ready to help if they need me, but I must wait for them to ask. My job is to be close, but not there. Yes, that's it, I will be close at hand, and hope and pray things will be okay and that I'm not needed.

Chapter Nine

Over the next several weeks, William traveled to different counties with Mitch, and he was shocked by the extent of Bobby's operation. Homeward was in the process of bidding on projects all over the state.

He wasn't learning much more in the way of quantitative evidence, but it did add qualitative insight. Homeward Enterprises was rapidly advancing throughout the state, and Mitch was connecting with subcontractors willing to sign on to the bid-rigging scheme. He never called it that, but William knew that's what was going on. Everyone talked using common phrases such as *You wash our hands, we'll wash yours. Don't worry, Bobby will make sure you are taken care of. This is how business is done.* The clichés were starting to make William nauseous. He knew from his experience as an auditor this was how some thought business had to be done to make it, but no matter how commonplace, if you get caught, it's still illegal.

He kept a log including the names of individuals they met with, companies they visited, dates, verbal agreements, and at times, cash changing hands. William had a few discussions with Mitch about what was transpiring, and Mitch confirmed that Bobby was building a network of contractors that worked together to streamline the bidding process and complete the building projects. He was never able to learn who inside the government was involved, but Mitch did tell him they had help from the inside.

William interacted with Mitch in a casual way leading him to believe William was fully on board and not at all uncomfortable with how they operated. He appeared to be enjoying his new role in the business, even started suggesting ways from an auditor's perspective that Homeward could do things that couldn't be traced. He wanted to make sure Mitch could see his acceptance of corrupt practices and increasing enthusiasm as Bobby threw cash his way.

William's skills of deception were tested at one point when Bobby stopped by his office and threw a large envelope on his desk.

"What's this," William asked as he broke it open and it revealed a stack of 100's. He looked up casually trying not to show any reaction.

"A little bonus for you, Billy. You been doin' a good job, Mitch tells me. I like it."

"Nice! Thanks." He put the envelope in his desk drawer as he displayed a sense of status quo and continued, "I've been wanting a few new things for myself, maybe a new watch or a couple nicer suits."

"Yeah, sounds good," Bobby answered and turned to exit. Then he stopped and turned in the doorway, saying as an afterthought, "Oh, Billy, I almost forgot. Take Joe Campa off the payroll. He's done."

"Sure thing, what happened? Did he quit?"

"No," Bobby said with a smile, "I canned him."

"Why? What'd he do?"

"He skimmed a little from cash we had him collect from one of our subs. We roughed him up a bit, and he gave it up, so he's gone."

"Gone? How gone?" William asked with slight concern.

"Relocated to another town, and we made sure he understands he better stay away and keep his mouth shut."

Bobby left, and William let out a gush of air as he was holding on to his breath for the last few moments of their conversation. He was relieved to learn Bobby didn't kill Joe but was beginning to understand what Bobby was capable of. It wasn't just illegal financial stuff, it was muscle to keep what was his. Hopefully, the same was true for Bobby's cousin, but with all the information his cousin had, he wasn't sure.

William took the cash Bobby gave him and bought a few high-end suits and a Rolex. He wanted to look the part, giving Bobby the false impression that he was hooked and his loyalty was strong.

As he met with Agent Breene each week, William filled him in on the trips with Mitch. They started altering their meeting places just as a precaution, and William was now authorized to keep Suzanne informed. Agent Breene noticed a change in William at one of their meetings.

"Wow William, nice watch and that suit – is it Italian?"

William responded with a laugh, "Thanks. Yes, Italian. Pretty slick, right?"

"Sure," Breene said with a slight scowl, "but why?"

"I don't know. I just thought I should act more like the sons. They dress like this, and Bobby has been giving me extra bonuses. I feel like I have to make sure Bobby doesn't have any doubts about me. The more time I spend with Mitch on the road, the more nervous I get thinking he's going to suspect something."

"I get it. You're smart, William. In more ways than one. Have you been easing into it?"

"Yes, because I didn't want to be the honest accountant one day and wake up the next day a crook. Sometimes Mitch wants to swing into a casino on our trips, and I have been doing a bit of gambling with him. I try to increase my stakes each time, and I've been asking him about betting on horses and sports, acting like I see him as my mentor. What a joke! I feel like an actor at times. This is so not me and never will be I can tell you that."

With a pat on William's back and a smile on his face, Agent Breene responded, "Good man, William. You know, you may have missed your calling. You would have made an excellent undercover cop."

"No thanks. I'm happy to say this is a temporary position."

After returning home from his latest trip with Mitch, William received a message from Agent Breene. He set up a meeting for Friday at 5:30 and told William to bring all the remaining documentation he had collected. William organized everything and put it into a file box. He was hoping this meant they were getting close to the end of the investigation as he was getting very anxious about continuing his deception with Mitch and Bobby.

With the file box in the back seat of his car, William drove to the meeting place. It was a rest stop ten miles out of town on the interstate. He parked at the end of the row, and soon Agent Breene's dark SUV pulled up and parked next to him. They both got out of their cars and walked over to a picnic table in the distance away from the parking area.

"Agent, Breene," William started, "I've collected all the documents I'd taken home and have organized my notes into spreadsheets and Word documents including my notes from the trips taken with Mitch. Everything is printed and saved on this flash drive."

"Thanks, William, I can take them. Your organization of the information is helpful. It's nice to have an accountant and auditor on the team. I wanted to meet with you today to tell you we're close to wrapping up this investigation and feel we have enough evidence with what you have for me today to bring Bobby in."

"What does that mean for me?"

"We have to get you out at the same time. Once we start questioning him and telling him we have evidence, he'll suspect you're involved."

"So.....how do you protect me....and my family?"

"We'll have a detail on all of you now, throughout the trial and until he is put away. These are serious charges, and he'll go to prison for a long time along with others."

"Can you tell me what the charges will be and who's involved," William asked.

"I'll tell you what I can. Let's put everything in my vehicle, then sit down and talk."

Agent Breene went through the long process of explaining what they had uncovered including evidence William provided as well as from other sources. The operation was headed up by Bobby, with several other construction companies involved in bid rigging, then there were suppliers and subcontractors involved in taking and paying bribes.

They were able to identify two persons inside, one responsible for the final decision on awarding contracts to build subsidized housing complexes and another responsible for grants and low-interest loans on other building projects.

The FBI felt Bobby was the one to go after along with the two State officials on felony charges of misappropriations of funds, collusion, and bribery. The suppliers and subcontractors would also be charged with lesser crimes, but most likely they would cut deals with them to provide evidence, and that would shore up the case against Bobby and the State officials nicely.

William paused in thought after Agent Breene finished. He felt Agent Breene was making some assumptions. He wondered how the FBI could be so sure Bobby would go to jail.

"What about before the trial? Will he get out on bail? And what if he doesn't go to jail at all, what if he's acquitted?"

"Don't worry about that now, William. We have a strong case, and we'll deal with the *what ifs* as they happen."

"I guess I can only hope that you know what you're doing here. I've put a lot of trust in you and the agency so far. All I can do is continue and finish what I started."

"Good attitude and, William, I can't tell you how much you've done for us. The bureau much appreciates your willingness to get involved. Without people like you, we would't be able to stop this corruption."

William smiled and said, "I can't say I was happy to do it. Hell, I've been scared to death at times, but I'm an honest man and do believe we need more people who will step up and do what's right."

Agent Breene then patted William on the back and said, "Now let's talk about what happens next. I wanted to meet with you today since it's Friday. Don't go into the office again. We'll pick Bobby up on Monday so I would suggest you take a personal day. We'll be there first thing in the morning, and at some point later in the week, will provide an escort for you to clean out your office.

"So that's it?" William asked. "We're done, and I no longer work for Bobby?"

"That's pretty much the size of it, but you knew this was coming, right?"

William got up from the picnic bench and paced back and forth a few times, scratching the back of his neck, then threw his arms up and said, "Okay, well I guess I just go home and tell Suzanne it's over….and start looking for a job."

Agent Breene took a breath, rubbed his hands together a few times and continued, "I hate to say this, but this is only the beginning. You should lay low for a while, maybe take the family on a little vacation. We have the evidence we need to arrest Bobby, but we may need you to testify, of course."

William sat back down. Shaking his head, he said, "I understand. I should have known it couldn't be this easy. Will you be in touch just as you have been throughout this whole ordeal?"

Agent Breene answered, "Yes, I certainly will and you'll see someone watching the house beginning today, Eleanor's too. In fact, someone is there now keeping an eye on Suzanne and Ellie. Just let me know if you decide to go out of town and let me know where you'll be. Remember you have my number and call anytime if you need me."

"So at this point, you don't know if I will need to testify?"

"No, we don't. It all depends on what develops after Bobby is arrested. The evidence you've given us may be all we need from you, but I can't say for sure. I'm sorry. I know the uncertainty is difficult to deal with and I hope you understand."

"I understand," William replied. "I don't like it, but I'm beginning to learn and accept the uncertainty that goes along with being involved in a criminal case as an informant."

After they said their good-byes, William got in his car and headed for home. He was anxious to get there now to make sure there truly was a security detail assigned to his house.

Chapter Ten

"Suz, I'm home," William shouted as he entered the house. "I have some good news." As they met in the living room, he hugged her then continued with more expression than was typical for him, "It's over. I gave Agent Breene everything I had, and I'm out of a job as of today."

"Oh....well...that's good, I think," she replied with some hesitation.

"I know the job part is weird, but the task of collecting information for the FBI is over. They have what they need. They'll be arresting Bobby Monday morning. Agent Breene told me not to report to work, to call in and take a personal day. Let's go out for dinner and celebrate."

"Is it really over? Can we relax now? I mean what about Bobby? How will he take being arrested?" She was clearly skeptical as William continued to make light of the situation.

"Who knows? Who cares? I have done my part, and I don't have to work with that criminal any longer. Let's consider this a new chapter in our lives, but just to be safe, Agent Breene does have a detail on us – purely precautionary, nothing to worry about. Once Bobby is arrested along with others involved, they'll make their case, and I can wash my hands of the whole matter."

He then moved to the kitchen to pour himself a drink, a slightly stiff one.

"Okay," she continued as she followed him, "If you say so. Uh, but why the early cocktail?"

"I'm celebrating. We've been through a lot - both of us. Join me?" he said as he lifted his glass and took a drink.

"No thanks. I'm not feeling as good about this as you are. I can't believe it's really over knowing there's someone from the FBI outside right now watching the house. Is there something you're not telling me?"

William turned his back on her so she couldn't see his face and headed towards the living room.

"No, nothing."

"William. Don't do this to me again. If there is anything you're not telling me...."

"Alright, you're right. Just one thing. It's over if the evidence I collected is enough. If not, I may have to testify, but it's just a small chance."

At that, she decided to pour herself a glass of wine, joined him on the sofa and said, "I get it. Makes sense. I'll just have to get used to my bodyguard out there and go with the flow."

"Suz, you are full of surprises. I thought that would upset you, but you are taking things in stride."

"At this point, what else can I do?"

"You may be right. By the way, where is Ellie?"

"Oh, she's with your mother. Eleanor wanted to take her shopping, and she thought you and I could use a night to ourselves. She's having Ellie stay overnight so we can relax and even sleep in tomorrow morning."

"Sounds good, but wait," he said as he jumped up and took his phone out of his pocket, "I have to makes sure they have protection."

"It's okay, Eleanor called and said she has her own detail as well so you can relax. So, now that we started drinking, we might want to order in instead of going out. What do you think?"

"I agree. Nothing fancy. How about pizza?"

"Works for me. I'll make the call."

When the pizza arrived, William opened a bottle of red wine – a Cab he had been saving for a special occasion. He decided this was as special as it gets. The last day he would work for a criminal, after working undercover so to speak, thrown into a situation he never thought he would find himself. Looking back he realized he had done some things that went completely against his nature. Lying on a daily basis at work was starting to become habitual, and he didn't like it.

"Hey Suz, I have a great idea. Let's take a trip. How about a cruise?"

"Sure. I've always wanted to do that and now would be a good time since you're not working, but what are you planning to do work wise anyway?"

"I was thinking I would take a break before I start looking. Maybe take on some clients and work from home for a while."

"That's not a bad idea," Suzanne replied.

"It shouldn't be hard to drum up some business, and I have put away quite a bit of money the past few years working for Bobby. He was always throwing bonuses at me. I think I'll sell this stupid Rolex."

"Good idea. I don't think I could ever get used to you in those fancy suits and that Rolex."

"I think Bobby thought the money would keep me quiet about his business especially after he started getting me more involved. It seemed like the more I learned about the business, the more money he paid me."

Suzanne laughed and shook her head saying, "Right. Hush money. He probably didn't even realize you had already become an informant."

"Informant," William said with a nod. "That's a word I never thought could end up on my tombstone."

"Ugh," Suzanne said with a shiver, "Don't even talk about that! Let's get back to your earlier thought. Where were you thinking of going on a cruise?"

"What would you say to a nice long trip, an Alaskan cruise?"

"Sounds good to me, but are there any restrictions from the FBI in case you do need to testify?"

"Agent Breene said to let him know if we leave town. He also said there would be months of preparation before the trial would start, even suggesting getting out of town for a bit might be a good idea."

Smiling she said, "Then it's settled, we embark on an Alaskan cruise as soon as possible. Should we ask Eleanor to join us?"

"Definitely," William replied

Eleanor was thrilled to join the family on their cruise, and with her along, William and Suzanne were able to enjoy some romantic dinners and late nights out while Ellie slept under the watchful eye of her grandmother.

One afternoon Eleanor and Suzanne relaxed by the pool while William played with Ellie in the water. They both watched for what seemed like hours as Ellie protested whenever her father suggested it might be time to get out of the pool.

"What a great time they're having," Eleanor said.

"Yes, they certainly are, and I think William is enjoying himself just as much as Ellie."

They sat quietly for several minutes, then Eleanor asked, "You look pensive, what are you thinking?"

"I was just thinking about how glad I am to have William as my husband and father to my child. It's such a gift."

"Your words express happiness, but your face tells me something different. If I'm not prying too much, is there something else?"

Suzanne frowned and said, "You read me well, Eleanor. I was also thinking about my childhood and the fact that I never experienced anything like this with anyone."

"I know you grew up in foster homes, but wasn't there ever a time when you went on a picnic or family vacation? Did you have any sort of father figure in any of the homes you lived in?"

"No," Suzanne answered, "I was never lucky enough to be placed in a home that felt like family or treated me like a member of the family for that matter. It wasn't that I was mistreated in any way, I really can't say that, but there was never any love. My basic needs were met, and I didn't stay in one home long."

"Oh dear, I'm so sorry. I understand why you see the relationship between William and Ellie differently than most moms would. You're happy for her, yet your memories of childhood make it sad for you at the same time."

"I'm not so sad for myself now, but it hurts to think about the child I was and what I missed out on and can never get back. I had no father or mother to love me. When I look at Ellie as each year passes, I think about myself as a child. I feel like we are two different beings, me as a child and me as an adult. I feel sorry for that child wishing a different life for her. Weird since I'm thinking about me."

"Was there ever a time you thought you could be adopted?"

"Yes, once. I was a teenager living with Mack and Lucy. They were an older couple. They had decided to take me in because she, like you, was a retired teacher and knew about the large numbers of kids in foster care and available for adoption in the county and wanted to give it a try. She had retired at fifty-five, but Mack was still working. She said he would probably work to the grave and she was a little lost."

"Doesn't sound like a very good reason to consider adopting a child."

"No, but kids in foster care have no choice and don't really care about the reasons, they just want a permanent home. Anyway, things went pretty well, and they were considering adopting me. I spent a lot of time with Lucy, but I didn't know Mack well. I always sensed he wasn't in total agreement with the whole idea."

"Did they have any children of their own?"

"Nope. They were sort of in the career slash couples group. They golfed, had cocktail parties, and took cruise vacations with other couples. Funny, here I am on a cruise. Anyway, Mack was a corporate exec and he traveled a lot for work, and even when he was home, he worked long hours. He was married to the job. I think that's why I was so excited when William took the job with Bobby's company and didn't have to work long hours."

"Didn't you bond with Lucy?"

"Not really," Suzanne said with a slight eye roll. "She was a nice enough person, but to her, I was just a project. She missed her students after she retired and Mack had no intention of giving her any more of his time, so she tried to use me to fill the emptiness retirement handed her."

"Is that why things didn't work out?"

"No, I believe they would have adopted me, and at some point, we could have formed a nice family unit, not the most loving kind like you, your husband, and William had, but it would have been better than anything I had up to that point."

"So what happened?"

"Mack got sick. It's that simple. He went for a routine test and found out he had cancer. It was curable, and his prognosis was pretty optimistic, but that was the end of me."

"Why, if his prognosis was that good?"

"Lucy wanted to devote all of her time and energy to taking care of Mack, and I was placed in another home. I only had about year left until graduation, so I stuck it out and then went to college, lived on campus, and since I was super poor, financial aid was available."

"Well that's something kind of good, I guess," Eleanor replied trying to think of something positive.

"I was able to stay on campus and work between semesters and, after graduation, I worked and lived in a small, but nice, apartment and I made a life for myself. It was a pretty happy time for me finally being on my own."

"All this time I've known you, Suzanne, you've never told me any of this. I mean we've spent a lot of time getting to know each other since you met William and I knew you grew up in foster care, but I never knew all of this. I'm sorry if I didn't seem interested."

"It's okay. I never wanted to talk about my childhood. It sucked."

Eleanor sat quietly taking it all in, then asked, "Do you know how you ended up in foster care? What happened to your parents?"

Suzanne paused, not sure she wanted to share, but then replied, "I was taken away from them when I was two years old, due to neglect. They were alcoholics. That's all I know, but in doing some research, learned the situation has to be pretty bad for that to happen. I chose not to learn anything further about my parents. I thought it would hurt too much."

Eleanor turned to face Suzanne and said with tenderness, "I know one thing for sure Suzanne, you may not have felt love as a child, but you know how to love, and you are a wonderful wife and mother.... and daughter-in-law to boot."

"Thanks for that. One thing I have learned is that you can't forget the past, but you can move away from it. My experiences will always be a part of me, but they don't define me. As you've gotten to know me, you know the person that started her life when she went to college, the person I am now."

"That's right, and I like her – a lot. Now, let's get ourselves a little frozen poolside drinky with a kick. What do you say?"

Suzanne laughed and said, "I say YES. Piña Colada for me."

After the family returned from the cruise, they spent a lot of time at home and at Eleanor's place. For a few weeks their lives were peaceful with little interruption, and while they all hoped it would come to a conclusion soon, they chose to take advantage of this period in a holding pattern and enjoy quality family time.

One Saturday afternoon, while Suzanne was busily preparing for Ellie's third birthday party, William received a call from Agent Breene.

"William, it's Agent Breene, how are you?"

"Fine, Sir, just fine. We've been staying close to home. How's the case going?"

"Things are moving right along, but there have been some new developments since we arrested Bobby."

"Oh? Like what?" William asked with more curiosity than concern.

"It's not something I can discuss with you over the phone. I'm going to need you to come down to our office. I'll send a car to pick you up. Can you come now?"

"Now? I... we are just about to have our daughter's birthday party. A few friends should be arriving within the half hour. Can't it wait?"

"Yes. How long is the party?"

"Just a couple of hours."

"How about I send a car at six? Will that work? It's very important, William."

William agreed and decided not to tell Suzanne until after the party. He didn't want to spoil the fun for her. She'd been so excited to have some friends over.

The party ended shortly after five and Eleanor was enjoying playing with Ellie and her new toys on the living room floor while Suzanne and William cleaned up.

"Hey, Suz? I have to talk to you about something."

"Sure, shoot."

"Agent Breene called this afternoon and needs me to come down to the FBI office. He said there are some new developments in the case. I'm sure it's nothing, he probably just wants to keep me informed. They're sending a car to pick me up at six. I'm sorry I have to leave soon, but he said it's important."

"Oh, that's fine. Your mom will help me get Ellie bathed and ready for bed. I'm sure she'll be sinking fast after her party. You go ahead, and when you get back, we'll share a bottle of wine, and you can fill me in."

She then gave him a hug and a kiss and continued with her cleanup.

After William left, Suzanne and Eleanor worked together to get Ellie settled down and ready for bed. They brought up some of the new books and stuffed animals for her. She was fast asleep in the middle of book two.

As they headed downstairs, Eleanor said, "I think I'll take off and get to bed early myself. Grandma is tired too."

"Sounds good and thanks for all the help today. Ellie had a wonderful third birthday, and you were a big part of that. We're so lucky to have you so close."

"You know I'm always happy to help and glad you let me be involved. I just love every minute!"

After Eleanor left, Suzanne turned down the lights, lit a few candles in the den and opened a bottle of Merlot. Just as she sat down with a magazine, she heard the garage door go up. *Perfect timing*, she thought.

"Hey, Suz. I'm back."

"Good, come sit down. I have your glass of wine already poured."

"Boy, I sure do need that. You won't believe what I've been through tonight. I don't even know where to begin." She could see the strain in his face.

"Is it bad? You look terrible."

"I'm trying to process it, but the main thing is they're pretty sure I'm going to have to testify, and that makes me nervous. If I have to sit in that witness box with Bobby looking right at me, I don't know if I'll be able to do it. The other thing is, this corruption may go much deeper than what I've been able to help them with."

"What do you mean?"

"I was able to give them a lot of circumstantial evidence like documents related to the bids, cash deposits, dates, telephone records, and things like that. Then I may have to testify with what they call more direct evidence like the conversations I had with Bobby, and the boys, and things I overheard especially on my trips with Mitch as he met with subcontractors and suppliers. The thing they're trying to get is direct evidence of collusion and bid rigging, trying to turn Bobby and maybe cut a deal with him. As one directly involved, he would provide the best testimony if he's willing. Turns out he's just a small part of this."

They continued to talk about William testifying, and both agreed since they had come this far, they would just have to get through it somehow no matter what turn of events occurred.

As they waited to hear when William would be called upon, they tried to keep life as normal as possible. William wasn't ready to look for another job, so he decided to use some of their savings and supplement that with working from home for a few small business clients. People knew he had worked for Homeward, but they assumed he just lost his job when Bobby was arrested. He was surprised when it seemed no one suspected him of any involvement in the illegal activities.

Chapter Eleven

Later that month, William received a call from someone at the district attorney office letting him know the trial was about to begin and he would need to meet with an attorney on the case to be briefed and prepped for his testimony. After several sessions, they felt he was ready and told him there were several days he would need to be in court to be called upon. The first day was a Wednesday the following week. A car would pick him up, and he requested that Suzanne be allowed to accompany him because she wanted to be there when he testified.

"Well, Suz, this is it. If I can just get through this trial, I'll be able to get on with my life. Excuse me - *we* will be able to get on with our lives."

"Right, we've been in this together."

"And have I told you how much I love you and that I appreciate your support through this whole ordeal?"

"Yes, you have, but it never gets old so tell me as many times as you wish."

The car was right on time, and Suzanne and William were on their way to the state capital for the trial. Eleanor arrived at the house bright and early to stay with Ellie, and as much as she was worried about William today, she was looking forward to some Grandma time with her little sweetie.

At the courthouse, Suzanne was escorted to the room where the trial would be held. She took a seat and anxiously waited for the trial to begin. William was taken to a room with other witnesses, and the assistant district attorney met with them to give them some information about the timing of things and also for some last minute instructions. They were reminded of things to remember when under oath and related to cross examination. William remembered most of it from his individual meetings with the DA's office personnel. He felt ready to get on with this and was happy Suzanne would be there to offer support.

After the briefing was done, they were left in the room to wait, and they were asked not to discuss the case with each other. Time seemed to stand still as they waited, but William kept checking his watch noticing more than two hours had gone by and nothing. Shortly after three hours, Agent Breene entered the room and crossed to William. He leaned down and quietly said in William's ear, "I need you to come with me, William."

William thought it must be time for him to testify, but wondered why Agent Breene was the one to get him. He thought it would be someone from the DA's office. It seemed like he had been handed off to them once Bobby was arrested and trial prep began.

Agent Breene didn't bring William to the courtroom, but he brought him to a small room at the end of a hall on a different floor and asked him to have a seat.

"William, I'm sure you're wondering what's happening. I brought you here because there's been a change, and I need to explain."

"That's fine, but where is Suzanne?"

"She'll be here soon, don't worry, she's fine, but I have to talk to you alone first."

"Is something wrong? You're scaring me."

"Let me explain. The trial has been canceled. The district attorney has agreed to a deal with Bobby. He's going to testify. You see, William, we were finally able to get Bobby to turn. He's been able to give us what we need to go after a whole chain of individuals involved in the corruption, and it's turning out to be bigger than we originally thought. It's not just bid rigging, it involves political campaign funds, and that means the government officials involved are part of something extremely corrupt. Bobby was just a pawn as he served in a way as a money launderer. Remember when I told you it could be just greed with bribes and kickbacks?"

"Yes. Did it turn out to be more?"

"Much more. Bobby and others in the group were funneling funds back into political campaigns including the Governor and others in his party. From what Bobby has told us, he didn't start this and is not the top guy. The Governor is, allegedly, and has been calling the shots. Bobby is running the bid rigging, and he and his group make out well financially, but the heart of the scheme is political financing from taxpayer dollars. Bobby isn't willing to go to jail for this, and he has testimony and his own file box of proof."

"But why now after all this time. I mean, right before the trial was about to start?"

"That's how it works in many cases. It takes the threat of the trial and real jail time for criminals to turn. Bobby thought it would never come this far and he was wrong."

"So it's over? You don't need me, or do you, for some other trial?"

"We'll still need you eventually, but things have changed considerably. Bobby's going to be a key witness, and we have to move him into the witness protection program. Have you heard of that?"

"Well, sure, I've heard of it, but don't know much about it."

"Unfortunately, we have to put you and your family in the program as well."

"I don't understand. Bobby is a criminal. Why doesn't he just make a deal for less time or something and why do I have to go into the program? I haven't done anything wrong!" William was starting to get angry.

"Try to stay calm, William. I'm sorry it's turning out this way. We honestly didn't expect this, but you never know with these corruption cases. Sometimes our initial investigation goes flat, and sometimes we uncover a deeper avenue of crime. Let me give you more information. We can take all the time we need."

"Yes, you better explain because I had no idea this was even possible," William replied, clearly agitated.

"What most people don't know is that more than ninety percent of the people in the program are criminals that have helped us put bigger criminals away. The average law abiding citizen like you in the program is rare. You just happened to be caught up in illegal activity, and now we need to protect you and your family."

"No, this is not what I want. I don't want my family anywhere near me. They won't be safe. Take me away somewhere, put me in the program, but keep me away from my family."

"I'm sorry, William," Agent Breene continued calmly, but firmly. "It's the only way we can keep you all safe. The three of you must have new identities and be protected as a unit. Let me get Suzanne, and you can talk about it with her. She needs to understand what's happened."

After Agent Breene finished giving William all the necessary information about how the witness protection program worked, Suzanne was brought in, and they were left alone to talk with an agent stationed outside the door.

After an initial hug, Suzanne said, "What's happening? Someone came in the courtroom and told us the trial was canceled due to some kind of settlement that was negotiated with Bobby."

"I know, Agent Breene brought me here to fill me in, and I have a great deal to tell you. I'm so sorry Suz, it's not good, and I'm still in shock."

He continued to explain all that had happened at his meeting with Agent Breene and that he was furious when told they would have to go into witness protection. He was under the impression that the information he gave the FBI would allow them to put Bobby away and that would be the end of it.

He told Suzanne how things had turned out quite differently with corruption leading all the way up to the Governor's office and crimes of collusion, misappropriations of funds, bribery, and political campaign funds.

Bobby was going to testify and hand over documents he had kept in his safe in order to protect himself should he get caught, but he would not be going to jail. He would go into witness protection, and therefore, William needed to go in as well.

He was confused at first until Agent Breene explained that Bobby was angry when he realized William must have ratted on him and he made threatening comments about William and his family. In the Program, Bobby would be free to go after William. They also feared others involved with much more to lose could go after William as well.

"So now what?" Suzanne asked.

"They said they wanted to give me some time with you to talk while they get things set up for us to be moved. Then they will take us home to get Ellie."

"Today?" she asked with tears in her eyes.

"Yes, today. They want to move us to a safe place, and I'll be brought back to testify, and then they'll set us up in a new place with new identities and a new job for me. He said I can't even be an accountant anymore. I have to do something different so it'll be harder for me....for us....to be found."

William paced, ran his hands through his hair, then rubbed his neck. He then turned to face Suzanne and said, "I don't want you and Ellie with me. I want to go alone."

She opened her mouth to speak, but no words would come.

He continued, "I mean it. I think you will be more at risk with me. I'm the one they'll go after, and I should be as far away from my family as possible."

He then sat down and put his head in his hands. Suzanne approached him and gently rubbed his shoulders. At first, she was mad and in shock, but now she realized he was beside himself.

"I understand how you feel, William, but we can't break up the family this way. The FBI will protect us, and Ellie is so young she won't remember any of this. Please, we have to stick together."

"I know we should be together, but I'm scared. I feel so guilty about getting us into this whole thing. I just want you and Ellie to be safe. That's all I care about!"

"Listen to me," Suzanne continued. "First of all, you didn't get us into this, it just happened, and you can't feel guilty about doing the right thing. Second, this is what we are facing, and we'll face it together."

"I understand how you feel, and I don't want to leave you, but it just seems like the best thing to do especially up until the time that I have to testify. I'm the one helping to put them away, so I'm the one at risk. You shouldn't be with me!"

"I'm serious about this. We will stay together. I'm not letting you go through this alone. Besides, the FBI seems to be insisting on it. They already have everything in place to put us in the Program with you, right?"

She was determined that William would see this her way and she was not backing down. He straightened his hair, took a deep breath and said, "Yes, good point. The FBI insists they can better protect the three of us together. They don't want to put me in the program alone, and I should trust they know what they are doing, but I just feel so helpless right now."

They hugged and remained silent for a few moments. Then William sighed and said, "Well, for better or worse, right?"

"That's right," Suzanne replied with a smile.

"Okay, we will all go into the Program as they recommend."

"What about Eleanor?" Suzanne asked.

"I'm not sure yet. Someone from the Witness Protection Program is coming in soon to go over everything in more detail. Agent Breene believes Mom will not be a target, but he said we can bring her into the Program with us if we want to and if she agrees. They rarely split up the immediate family within one household, but extended family members are optional. He said they have flexibility there. In Eleanor's case, it's up to her."

Over the next couple of hours, Suzanne and William met with an agent in the Program and learned how things would happen. They were each given a file of information with their new names and some background information. William would be placed in a new job, and they would live in an apartment in a different town. After the trial and about a year's time, they would be free to purchase a home if they wished.

William was able to call Eleanor and let her know they would be home late that evening and that the trial had been called off. He told her he would have to explain everything when they got home. She could sense the strain in William's voice, but she knew this wasn't the time to question him. She had to wait for him to explain.

After putting Ellie to bed, she turned on the television and found an old movie to watch hoping it would help to pass the time. As the evening hours passed she dozed on and off on the couch in the den until the doorbell rang. She approached the door with caution, but knowing security was watching the house, felt she would be safe. To her surprise, the two men at the door were FBI agents.

"Mrs. Gable?"

"Yes....has something happened?" she asked as her heart began to race.

"May we come in?"

"Of course, please. We can go into the living room and sit down."

"We're here to inform you that your son and daughter-in-law were in a serious accident on their way home from the courthouse," one of the agents began.

"How serious? Are they going to be okay?"

"We don't have any details at this time on their conditions, but have been instructed to bring you to the hospital where they were taken by ambulance."

"Yes, of course, I understand. I'll call a friend to come and stay with my granddaughter."

Eleanor made the call, and after her friend arrived, she gathered her coat and purse and left with the agents who drove her to the hospital.

After spending several hours at the hospital, one of the agents drove her home the next morning - alone. Both William and Suzanne were gone, and she would have to raise her granddaughter on her own.

She was overcome with grief, but she would have to put that aside and focus on what had to be done. Eleanor had faced challenges in her life, but this proved to be the most difficult. She was strong and determined, but there were times when she had to dig deep to find the strength and courage to keep going.

After selling William and Suzanne's house, she moved Ellie to her home. She would raise her there where she knew William and Suzanne would approve. She remembered they had talked about buying their next house outside of the city, closer to William's childhood home in preparation for expanding the family with another child.

There were moments of sadness for Eleanor in the quiet of the night while Ellie slept, giving her time to reflect on all that had happened. Living out her days without her son and daughter-in-law in her life sometimes seemed unbearable. If not for Ellie, she didn't know how she would have overcome her grief.

The first few months were heart wrenching as Ellie cried herself to sleep most nights. At her age, it was impossible for her to understand why her parents were no longer with her. Eventually, she adjusted to her new life with Eleanor and the memories of life with her parents faded, but Eleanor was determined she would always talk about William and Suzanne to ensure Ellie knew what loving parents she had and where she came from.

She kept family photos displayed throughout the house and in albums. She and Ellie talked about Mommy and Daddy as they looked at the photos. She insisted Ellie refer to her as Grandma El, never wanting to replace Suzanne who would always be Ellie's mother.

As she put Ellie to bed one night, she watched her drift off to sleep after their ritual of reading three of her favorite books. Her thoughts returned to the night of the accident. *All the years Suzanne and William will miss seeing their little girl grow up. Could it have been different? If only they had made different choices. Or, I wonder, was this out of our control, merely our fate?*

Part Two

Layton

Chapter Twelve

Layton Virnetti entered the outer office of her law practice early Monday morning. She was eager to start the day working on a new case with a client involved in a hit and run accident over the weekend. Layton had been practicing law in her home town for the past few years after leaving Hampton, Hampton, and Mills, Attorneys at Law, in New York City. Interning at a big firm in the City was her dream, and she was thrilled to have the opportunity each summer during her years at law school to clerk at the firm.

She worked hard hoping to secure a position after graduation. Her hard work paid off, and she was offered a permanent position in the corporate defense department. The cases she worked on involved big companies being sued for a wide variety of complaints such as product liability, environmental concerns, and employment rights violations.

She knew she had to start at the bottom in a big firm, but she wasn't prepared for how her level of disappointment grew each month incrementally in her job. The experience was enlightening in many ways. The learning experience respective to the law was unmatched, but she also learned how disadvantaged the other parties could be up against a large corporation represented by a firm like Hampton, Hampton, and Mills.

After just eighteen months, she decided to make a change and applied for a position in the public defender's office in the county where she grew up. The offer came swiftly given her credentials and the fact that the pay was low and the caseload heavy. She needed to see things from a different perspective and felt her assumptions about what she wanted to do with her law degree may have been all wrong. Again, the experience demonstrated to her what she didn't want in her career rather than what she wanted. As a public defender, she worked with clients that were often guilty, and the caseload made it impossible for her to provide services to her clients at the level of expertise she expected from herself. Guilty or not, she did believe each and every client deserved her best effort and the best possible defense, but she found she did not enjoy representing those who were guilty of their crimes.

The next step was to open her own office in her home town affording her the ability to accept the cases she chose to accept and to develop the practice by her design. She specialized in defense of clients she believed to be innocent, with some ability to pay, and a sincere desire to assist her in preparing their case. She expected cooperation and a positive attitude from her clients.

At first, it was difficult, financially. She lived with her parents for six months and invested all of her savings into the office. She found it necessary to include ancillary services such as preparing wills, reviewing contracts, and facilitating real estate transactions, just to pay the bills and begin to build a client base.

Today the case she would begin to prepare was right in her wheel house. Janice Kemp was arrested on Saturday for leaving the scene of an accident. It happened Thursday evening, and she claims she didn't even know she hit someone. Layton believed her and would meet with her today at Janice's home.

"Hello Janice," Layton said as her newest client opened the front door.

"Miss Virnetti, please come in. I just made a pot of tea. Would you like some?"

"Yes, I would. Call me Layton. Can we sit at the dining room table to talk? I need to take some notes and have a few papers to go over with you."

"Sure, Layton, whatever you need. Just make yourself comfortable in the dining room, and I'll get the tea."

Janice was obviously a little dazed and looked as if she hadn't slept well the past few nights. Layton knew that was a sign of her innocence.

After returning with the tea, Janice sat quietly across from Layton at the table, saying nothing as she waited for Layton to lead the conversation.

"Janice, I know you've given me information about the arrest, but let's go over things again so that I can make sure I have a clear understanding of what happened. Can you begin when you left your house on Thursday, and tell me everything you remember about that night?"

"Yes. Well, I left the house at about 6:30 with my book bag and umbrella. It was supposed to rain sometime in the evening. I drove to the bookstore in town. It takes about 20 minutes, but I like to get there a little early and talk with people before our group starts. The book discussion was just like every other week. We talk about the book we are reading, have a glass of wine or two, and wrap up around nine. Some of the girls stay and chat or go across the street to the sports bar for a nightcap, but I left as soon as the discussion ended because it was starting to storm, and I had an early meeting in the morning."

"Was it raining hard?"

"Not so much when I left, but it got worse as I made my way down route 31."

"Was it dark yet?"

"Yes, it was very dark. The storm clouds must have made it worse."

"Go on. Tell me what happened as you were driving home."

Janice hesitated, seemingly upset just thinking about the drive home that night, so Layton poured her a little more tea then said, "It's okay, Janice. I'm not here to judge you. Just tell me what happened and we'll go from there."

Janice took a sip of tea, a deep breath, then continued, "After I left the bookstore, as I said, it started to rain harder, and it was difficult to see, so I went pretty slow. There were no other cars on the road, and I was glad of that. Things were going alright until I got out of town. I was driving on thirty one past the Wilson Farm, you know on that stretch that sort of twists and turns."

"Yes, I know it well. It scares me sometimes even in the daylight," Layton said as she tried to reassure Janice.

"Just as I was coming to one pretty sharp turn in the road, a deer jumped out from the woods and ran in front of me. I wasn't going very fast and he almost got past me, but I hit him in the back end with the corner of my car. It was so loud that I thought I must have killed him, but as I looked to my left, I could see he stumbled a little in the road, got back on his feet, then went running off into the woods on the other side."

"And what did you do then?"

"I pulled over to the side of the road to catch my breath. It really scared me, and I wasn't sure what to do. I thought about it for a few minutes and decided I wasn't going to get out of the car for any reason. Not on a dark, rainy night like that out there in the middle of nowhere."

"Yes, that would be dangerous."

"After I calmed down, I figured it would be okay just to drive home as long as my car was drivable and the deer took off, so it wasn't lying in the middle of the road or anything. So I went home."

Janice then started to tear up and said with angst, "Oh Layton, I had no idea. And to think of that poor man, I just don't know how I could possibly have hit him. I swear I never saw him, just the deer."

"It's going to be alright, now. Let's keep going. I have some questions, and please try to understand this is only going to help me prepare your defense. Take nothing personally."

"I understand," she said as she wiped her eyes with a napkin.

"You said there was wine at the book store for your group. Did you have any?"

"Yes, one glass. I usually have two, but with the weather and all, I thought I'd better stick to one."

"That's good. Do you think anyone could verify that?"

"I don't know, probably not. I'm sure no one pays much attention to how much anyone is drinking. No one goes overboard."

Layton finished taking a few notes and then continued with her questions, "Let's move on to what you did after you got home."

"Okay, so when I got home, I put my car in the garage, and then I checked out the front of the car to see how much damage there was before going inside. I saw some blood, but not much. I guess the rain washed most of it away. Oh, and there was a little fur stuck in the grill on the front of the car."

"What about the next day? Tell me what you did the next day, Janice."

"I called my insurance company first thing, and they said they needed to take some pictures of the damage and asked if I could come down to the office. I went over during my lunch hour and then I ran the car through the car wash."

"Are you sure of that? You went to the car wash after the pictures were taken and not before?"

"Yes, absolutely sure. I thought it was best they saw the fur so they would know I hit a deer and didn't hit another car."

Layton finished the last few drops of her tea then started to pack up her things.

"Very good, Janice. I have what I need for now. I'll do some work at the office and review the police report to see if I can get some additional details from them. I also want to talk to the book store owner and some of the others in your group. I think we can prepare a nice defense for you. They will say you were drinking and didn't want to be charged with driving under the influence and that's why you left the scene without contacting the police. They'll try to discredit your claim that you only saw the deer. We can counter all of that."

"How can we? Isn't it just my word?"

"No, we have a lot to work with. There are many things about your behavior that support innocence rather than guilt. For example, you called your insurance company and let them take pictures *before* washing the car. If you were guilty, you would have washed the car right away and probably wouldn't have turned it into your insurance company at all. Then we can do some checking about the deer. The insurance pictures may show the fur in the grill.

Try not to stress too much. There's a good chance we will get these charges dropped.

"I hope you're right."

"Can we go out to where it happened in the next day or two so that I can take a look?"

"Sure. How about tomorrow after work? I was too upset to go in today, but I'll be working tomorrow."

"Works for me. I'll be in touch, Janice. Get some rest, I'm sure this has been worrisome for you."

Layton worked the rest of the day in her office on Janice's case. In reading the arrest warrant, she learned that a fifty six year old man had been hit by a car in that same stretch of road on Thursday night. He was found dead around 10 PM when a passerby saw his body off the right side of the road. He suffered multiple injuries including a head injury that may have occurred when his head hit a rock upon landing. It was a preliminary report, and a full autopsy would be performed, one that included a full tox screen to determine if there was any alcohol or drugs in his system. Layton definitely wanted to see that report once it was available.

She was interrupted by a phone call that she answered with, "Layton Virnetti." Silence. "Hello, this is Layton Virnetti, may I help you?"

Hesitantly the man on the other end said, "Um, yes. I need your help. I...well you see...my wife, no ex-wife, she's trying to take my kids away ... for good."

"I'm sorry to hear that. Let's start with your name."

"My name is Richard Wilson. A friend of mine gave me your name. He said you helped him with his divorce and you were very good."

"Hello, Richard. Please call me Layton. Now, do you want to give me more information over the phone or would you like to come to my office and talk?"

Layton then proceeded to set up a time for them to meet. They agreed on 5:30 that evening when he got out of work. She sensed he didn't want to wait to see her. He seemed anxious to tell her what was going on, and he needed to be reassured that she could help him. Working into the evening was a normal practice for her. It was two-fold. First, it helped to be flexible with peoples' schedules, and then it allowed her to see people right away when she felt it necessary. This case definitely felt necessary.

Continuing to work on Janice's case while she waited for Richard to arrive, she printed the list of names in attendance at the book store that Janice had emailed her earlier and started making phone calls.

"Hello."

"Yes, may I speak to Karen?"

"This is she."

"This is Layton Virnetti. I'm working with Janice from your book discussion group, and I have a couple of questions for you."

"Questions? Why?"

"It seems Janice was involved in an accident Thursday night driving home from the meeting and..."

"Oh no, is she alright?"

"Yes she's fine, but she hit a deer, and in that same stretch of road, a man was hit and killed."

"You don't mean the hit and run I heard about on the news?"

"Yes. Now, would you be willing to answer a few questions."

"Sure. If I can."

"Do you remember seeing Janice at the meeting?"

"Yes, she was there. I talked to her quite a bit."

"Did she stay for the entire meeting?"

"Yes, but she left as soon as it ended. I remember because she was concerned about the weather."

"Do you recall if she had any wine?"

"Sure did, I poured her a glass myself."

"Did she have more than one glass?"

"No."

"Are you sure?"

"I'm absolutely sure. I got up to get myself a refill and asked her if she wanted more, and she said she didn't. She was worried about the weather. She said she better stick to just one glass."

"Did she usually drink more at other meetings?"

"Why so interested in her drinking? What's happening here? Is Janice in trouble?"

"I'll be honest, Karen. They have charged her with leaving the scene of an accident. I can't give you any more information than that, but I am representing her. You're being very helpful so can we go on?"

"Of course. I'm sorry. I understand you being her attorney and all."

"Thanks. So can you tell me if you know how much she typically drank at your meetings?"

"Oh, I'm not sure, but she never seemed to go all out. I think she would have two, three glasses tops, but as I said, that night it was only one that I was aware of."

"How long did the meeting last?"

"Two hours, just like clockwork. We have a set time frame because the book store closes and the owner doesn't like to stay late. Some of the girls go out after, but Janice never did. She wanted to be fresh for work in the morning."

"Do you know if anyone else left when she did, maybe someone drove in the same direction from the bookstore?"

"I don't know, not that I noticed."

"Well, I think that's all I need, Karen. Thank you so much for talking with me."

"You're welcome. I like Janice. I hope everything works out, and if I can be of any more help, let me know."

Layton connected with three more in attendance Thursday night and with the bookstore owner. The information she gathered was in line with what Janice had described. She felt confident Janice was truthful about the timeline and the alcohol.

Richard Wilson arrived at Layton's office at 5:30 on the dot. In her mind, being prompt was a sign of a client's innocence. It wasn't definitive, but it became one of the pieces she used as she formed an opinion of the client's character.

"Richard," she said as she offered her hand, "good to meet you. I'm Layton." He shook her hand, and she noticed it was damp with sweat.

"Thanks for seeing me so soon. I'm a little nervous about this whole thing. I've never hired a lawyer before."

"I guess you could say that's a good thing," Layton said with a smile. "Please sit down, and we'll get started. I ordered a couple of sandwiches from the Deli. I thought since you were coming right from work, you might be hungry."

Layton opened a brown bag that was sitting on her desk, set one sandwich in front of him and another in front of her. She then added a few napkins and a couple of bottles of water.

"Oh, sure," he replied, "that's so nice of you. I'd like that. Thanks."

"Now, how about you start at the beginning and tell me what lead up to your needing a lawyer."

Richard then began his story as they ate their sandwiches. He had been divorced for about three years, and in the original divorce agreement, he and his ex-wife agreed on joint custody. Things had been pretty amicable between them until six months ago when she announced she was getting married and wanted to leave the area, taking the kids with her.

He talked about his girls and how much he would miss them if they lived so far away. Tears brimmed in his eyes when he brought out school pictures from his wallet.

Layton dug into the details by asking questions about the man his ex-wife planned to marry, and she learned his ex-wife had met him on-line. To her surprise, Richard had not yet met the man. His ex-wife had been cooperative throughout the divorce and sharing custody had been working well until recently. She seemed to be acting impulsive and reckless.

This one seemed like a slam dunk once they got to the courtroom, but Layton feared Richard's ex-wife was at risk for doing something stupid in the meantime. She would need to be careful with this one.

"Richard, I have the information I need to get started, and I will take your case. Can you get me a copy of your divorce agreement, and I have a form I would like you to sign giving me permission to speak with the lawyer that handled the divorce."

"I can get you a copy, but like I said, I've never hired a lawyer. My ex-wife and I did the agreement ourselves off one of those legal sites on the internet. The papers were signed and notarized, but we didn't have anyone representing either one of us. Sorry, is that a problem?"

"Not to worry. Just get me the copy, and I'll review it and get started on your case. Now, do you think your ex-wife is also consulting with an attorney?"

"I doubt it. It seems like she's getting orders from the guy she's about to marry."

"Okay, well that's good. Can you get me any information about him? Just his name, where he lives or works, anything like that would be helpful."

"I hate to involve the girls, but they may be able to tell me something to get me started. I get them off the bus on Fridays because I work four, ten-hour days and have Fridays free. I'll go a little early next time and see if I can snoop around the house a little and find anything."

Layton took a slow breath before giving him a final caution.

"Richard? Just one last thing I want to tell you. Be on your toes. If you notice any behavior from the girls or your ex-wife that seems odd, let me know right away. Influence from a third party like this fiancée could make her do something unexpected. I don't want to alarm you..."

"It's okay, I get it. I'm worried about all sorts of things like her up and taking the kids without telling me. That's why I thought I'd better get a lawyer. Thanks for seeing me on such short notice. I'll get you whatever you need." At which point he developed a look of sheer determination and added, "I can't lose my kids! I'll be watching her like a hawk."

Chapter Thirteen

"Hi, Dad," Layton said with a smile as her father opened the front door."

"There's my girl. How many times have I told you – *You don't have to ring the bell.* This was your home for what, over twenty five years?"

"I know, I know, but since I moved to my own place, I feel funny just using my key. Where's Mom?"

"She's over at Ruby's having coffee. Should be home soon, so I guess you're stuck with me for now."

Layton went straight for the kitchen counter and sat in her usual stool. Her father, Hank, put on the tea kettle and moved the cookie jar in front of her. This was their ritual since she was little. Neither of them could resist the cookie jar, and this was how they shared many Saturday afternoons talking.

"So, how's the law office shaping up? Getting any new clients?" Hank asked.

"Yes, actually, I am. Not more than I can handle yet, but this move to open up on my own is proving to be enough to earn a living."

"All paying customers so far, I hope."

"Yes, Dad, don't worry. No pro-bono come anockin' at my door yet," she said with a laugh. "I did turn one down last week, though."

"Oh yeah, why's that?"

"Shady character. Didn't believe he was innocent so I sent him packing."

"What'd he do?"

"This guy came in all acting like he was the boss over me, telling me what I was going to do for him and you know that doesn't sit well with me from the start. He said the State was after him for unpaid sales tax. Said they assessed him on sales he never made and they were charging outrageous penalties and fees. I did a little checking and found out this wasn't the first time he's been in trouble for not paying taxes. Not just sales tax, but payroll taxes, income taxes, you name it, he tried to avoid paying it."

Hank shook his head and said, "Some guys never learn, do they?"

"Nope, and I found out he goes to a different lawyer every time he's in trouble. He was shocked when I told him I wouldn't take his case. I think he thought I was a pushover."

"He was wrong there. You may look young, and might I add very beautiful, but underneath it all you've always been able to handle the tough stuff. I'm glad you turned that case down. You did the right thing."

"Thanks, Dad. I know I need to pay the bills, but I don't need to get rich on this gig. I want to stay true to my beliefs, you know, be able to sleep at night knowing I haven't compromised my ethics."

They sat quietly for a few minutes and then Hank decided to ask the question he really wanted to ask, from the moment she walked in the door.

"How's the other case going? You know, with Arthur?"

She paused and took another cookie.

"Not well. It's been difficult."

"Yes, honey, I know, but are you getting anywhere with him?"

"Not with his help."

"That's too bad. I can't understand it."

"I know, but in a way, I can. He's always been a super private guy. All these years I've known him, yet I don't know much about him at all."

"What are you going to do? How will you build his case?"

Layton tilted her head to the side and gave a little smirk.

"I have my ways. I'll build him a defense with or without his help, and I know that goes against all I've said when describing what I want in a client, but he means too much to me. I won't give up on him. I know he's innocent."

Earlier that month -

"Arthur, I want to help you, but you have to give me more to work with. You've been accused of a crime, and I'm here to defend you, but I can't do that if you continue this refusal to give me any information. What happened? Why is everyone so sure you are guilty of embezzlement?"

Layton pleaded with her client as she visited him for the third time in the client visitation room at the county jail. Her frustration was mounting with each visit and, as he had done each time before,

Arthur offered her nothing that would help. He simply replied calmly and slowly, "I didn't do it, that's all I can say. Just defend me the best you can. I trust you to do your best. That's it. I'm sorry."

"If you trust me, you can talk to me. I need to know more about you, some history. Details about your past and we'll need some character witnesses. I know you didn't do this. I know you aren't capable of this crime, Arthur. That's just not you, but they must have some real evidence to use against you, or it would never have gone this far."

She leaned in towards him as she spoke each pleading word, her eyes fixed upon him, unwavering, yet he remained unresponsive as he looked down at his hands resting in his lap.

Layton sighed, picked up her notepad, put it in her briefcase, closed the case, motioned for the guard to unlock the door and left without another word.

Arthur looked up and watched as she walked away. As soon as she was out of sight, he put his elbows on the table, covered his face with his hands and took one deep breath, letting it out with force. He knew he was in for a difficult road ahead, and this would not be the last trying conversation with Layton. He desperately wanted to give her what she asked for, but he was not in a position to do that, and it hurt because he cared for her in a way she would never understand.

After leaving the jail, Layton returned to her office, poured a cup of coffee and opened Arthur's file, trying to find some way to represent a client that wouldn't give her anything to work with to properly prepare his defense. She wasn't even sure where to start.

In her experience, the place to start was with your client. Those first few discussions with a client could be very helpful. She thought of them as information gathering sessions, and the client was often surprised by the types of questions she would ask, finding it difficult to understand how some things could be important. A skilled attorney knows what to ask and why, but this was a first for Layton, her client wouldn't talk.

More than a first, it was like a blow to the head because she didn't see it coming. Having known Arthur for so many years, she thought he would be one of the least resistant and would gladly offer information once under the client/attorney confidentiality protection. How wrong she had been.

As she drank her cup of coffee she thought, *I'm the only person in town that would defend him and I'm pretty sure the only one that believes he's innocent. I don't just believe he's innocent, I'm sure of it. I realize now after this recent meeting with Arthur that I have to step into the role of detective and find out about his past so that I can provide him with a strong defense and win this case. He might not approve, but I'll have to do it, in my client's best interest. I swore to defend my clients to the best of my ability, and I'm going to do whatever it takes to do that for Arthur.*

She had known Arthur for almost twenty years. She remembered the day he moved into the house on her block, arriving in a black SUV pulling a small U-Haul trailer. Two men were with him and, after they helped him unload the trailer, they left in the SUV. She never saw the two men again, and over the years she didn't remember Arthur ever having visitors at the house.

That was on a Saturday. On Monday after dinner Layton overheard her father tell her mother that he had learned the man started working at the only real estate office in town. It was a small office with just two real estate agents and one broker. Arthur became the third of the agents, and since Belmont was a small town in a rural area, there wasn't much going on in the way of property sales.

Her father said that he wondered why they would need to add another agent. He didn't feel there was much work for the two agents currently working there, but as he told her mother, he knew there was a lot of undeveloped land in the county, so it was possible there were plans in the works that he wasn't aware of. Developing more underutilized land would improve the tax base, and that could be beneficial for everyone.

Arthur Bowles was his name, and she met him for the first time walking to school one day shortly after he moved in. She was walking on the sidewalk in front of his house when he came out of his front door. He was walking to work in the same direction as the school, and she introduced herself as his neighbor that lived a few houses away and finished by asking his name. He seemed reluctant to tell her.

She sensed a strange hesitation before he finally said, "My name? My name is Arthur. Yes, Arthur ... Bowles." It even seemed to her to be a question rather than a statement.

She replied, "Hi Arthur. I'm Layton, and I guess we are neighbors now."

They walked together the rest of the way to her school. His real estate office was just a short distance past the school. They didn't talk much, but she sensed he was happy to have a companion on his walk to work.

When they reached the school, Layton said, "It was nice to meet you, Arthur."

"Have a nice day Layton," he replied and then continued on.

For the next few years, they would walk together periodically and pass the time talking. The conversation was relaxed as he asked her about school, friends, and her other interests. He was a good listener, and she began to also rely on him for counsel and advice especially when it came to important decisions such as what career to pursue and where to attend college, but they didn't talk much about him. He avoided the subject, and she respected his wishes to remain a mystery. Layton learned early on he was a private man who didn't want to share details of his past and she accepted that.

Unfortunately, the adults in the community were much more judgmental. Arthur kept to himself with a majority of his interactions with locals limited to his work, with very little on a social level. This caused people to talk, and many viewed him as odd, unfriendly, even rude. As a young girl, Layton was bothered by this, and it led to her mature approach in her interactions with Arthur. She accepted him as a private man and grew to like him very much.

She remembered her first impression of Arthur. He was a good looking man with strong features. His dark curly hair always seemed to be a mess, as if he chose to just let it take on a look of its own. He rarely went to the barber, she guessed about twice a year. His face looked like that of a man much older than he really was like his face displayed something he had endured at a young age. She could never put her finger on it, but she thought he must have experienced some tragedy or sadness in his life. You could see that in his face, but his eyes told a different story. They were a deep blue, and when he looked at her, she saw that whatever he had endured hadn't affected his eyes. They were kind and compassionate, something Layton believed very few recognized as they continued to avoid the stranger in town assuming he was unsociable, unapproachable. Layton, however, believed Arthur to be a caring, thoughtful man. She had been good at sensing the quality of a person's character from a young age even without knowing much about him, she had a good sense of the type of person he was.

Yet now she wished he had revealed more to her about his life particularly before moving here, but he didn't so she found herself in a difficult situation trying to defend a man she knew little about. She felt she knew his heart, now she needed more than that, she needed details. This had gone beyond casual friendship, their relationship had moved into a more serious phase, one of attorney and client and his future depended on it.

And now, as she sat in her office finishing the last of her coffee she thought, *I'm feeling so distressed about his predicament. It hurts to think about it because I really care about him. I feel so frustrated by his silence, and I know I have to find out what possessed him to keep quiet. What is he hiding? What is he afraid to reveal even to me?*

Then she started to expand her thoughts to those of doubt. *Could I be wrong about Arthur? If he is hiding something, could that mean he is guilty? I don't know much about him, so I suppose I could be wrong about him and he could have something in his past that would hurt his case. Have I been wrong about him all these years, believing he was a good, honest man who just doesn't like to talk about himself? My belief that he cared about me and our friendship, have I been naive, deceived? I can't think this way, I have to go with my gut and believe him, but at the same time, I have to find the truth no matter what that truth may turn out to be.*

Chapter Fourteen

After Layton left, Arthur returned to his jail cell and sat on his cot thinking. *This can't be happening to me. I'm innocent, but no one believes me except Layton. She's the one person I can rely on, but she's also the one I'm hurting the most by not telling her what she needs to know. Yet I can't, I just can't tell her about my past. It would put her in danger, and I'm not going to do that. I have to stay strong and have faith that this will be resolved, I'll get through this trial and found innocent of these charges so that I can go back to my quiet life.*

He had a lot of time to think since being arrested. Layton was working to secure bail so that he could be released until his trial, if it ever came to that. He knew she was an excellent lawyer, and given the right tools, she could give him a good defense and maybe even avoid going to trial. She could get the charges dropped due to insufficient evidence, and things would return to normal. She had done it before for her clients on similar charges, but he also knew this was different. She didn't have much to work with. His silence was putting up a barrier for her, but he felt he had no choice.

As he thought about Layton, he remembered the first day they had met. She was walking by his house just as he was coming out onto the sidewalk. He had just passed through an opening in the tall hedge that lined the front yard. He had not seen her coming and felt he would be all alone on his walk to work, something he hoped for each day as he ventured out of his house.

He wasn't comfortable interacting with neighbors. He feared people would pry and he wasn't at all interested in talking about himself or his life before moving to town. He had experienced so much pain. He wanted to keep to himself as he highly valued his privacy.

It wasn't that he was unsociable or impolite, it was just that he had to be cautious. He had to be deliberate in what he said, and that took a great deal of effort, he found it tiring. But it was different with Layton. From the first day they met and walked together, he knew she was special. At first, she would ask him about himself, but as he avoided her questions, she quickly realized he didn't wish to reveal much to her and she respected that. For someone her age, he thought that said a lot about her, and he quickly realized he could let himself become friends with Layton. As a young girl, she was so unassuming and nonjudgmental. She was mature in her thinking, and while at first, she was curious about him, she wasn't meddlesome and didn't pry into unwelcome territory.

She was happy to discuss her life and often times asked him for his advice. She found it easier to tell him things that she wasn't comfortable talking to her parents about and he was happy to listen and help her think through things and come to her own decisions.

Now he would have to find a way to help her prepare his defense with things he could tell her about what has happened since moving to town, at the same time staying away from events that happened in his previous life. At their next meeting, he would attempt to make her realize the past was not relevant to his case. He wasn't sure how he would do it, but because he knew deep in his heart that she believed in his innocence, he would find a way.

Armed with a large double shot latte, Layton began the process of finding out as much as she could about her client, Arthur Bowles. She started with the low hanging fruit, a good old internet search of public records. Many would be surprised to learn how much information is out there and all you need is a device with access to the internet. She subscribed to a service that searches all public records and spits back a comprehensive report on the individual in a matter of minutes. The report would include anything found including birth, death, marriage, divorce, arrests, property deeds and assets, relatives, current and past addresses, court and criminal records, aliases, judgments, bankruptcies and tax liens, and various amounts of business data.

Also accessible were things related to what a person reveals through social media, however, she doubted she would find much in Arthur's case, he didn't seem like the type to engage socially on the internet, but she could be wrong. The only records not included in the report would be those that were sealed such as juvenile records, confidential agreements, and jurors and material witnesses in some court cases.

After typing in his full name, current city and state of residence and approximate age, the site went to work and came back with a report more quickly than she had expected. After opening the report on her screen she understood why. It was one of the smallest reports she had ever generated.

Her initial thought was, w*ow not much to work with here - birth certificate, high school graduation place and* *year, real estate license, automobile registrations, and just one relative, mother – Claire Bowles.*

She took another look at the birth record closely and found that he had been born in San Francisco, California, and he was in his early fifties. His mother's name was listed, Claire Bowles, but his father's name stated - unknown. She paused. *Now, this is interesting. Arthur was born to a single mother, and he was born in California. I'm surprised he never mentioned being raised by a single mother, but then again I shouldn't be surprised at all since he didn't share much about his life.*

As she continued to look through the small report, she was perplexed not by what she found, but by what she didn't find. Not even one misdemeanor. No judgments or bankruptcies. Arthur was squeaky clean. It wasn't very telling, but then in her preparation of his defense, she would be sure to emphasize this embezzlement charge as his first offense and his clean record supported the presumption of innocence. Then she reminded herself the district attorney's office would counteract with the premise that this only proves he wasn't caught doing any illegal acts and that he may have committed other crimes that he was able to conceal. Even go so far as suggesting he was an expert at deception.

Her research was interrupted by a knock. The door to her office was half opened, and she could see a gentleman looking in. He was tall and thin wearing a dark suit and tie. He cleared his throat before saying, "Miss Virnetti?"

"Yes," she replied. "Can I help you?"

"My name is Burch, Detective Burch, from the county Sherriff's office. I understand you're representing Arthur Bowles." She waited for him to continue, but he hesitated in the doorway to her office, and she realized he was waiting for a response.

"Yes, I'm representing Arthur Bowles. Please come in, have a seat. Would you like some coffee?"

He moved slowly into her office, took a seat at one of the chairs in front of her desk and replied, "No thank you, I'm fine. I just have a few questions I'd like to ask you." Then he looked around her office as if he were making mental notes. He took out a small pad of paper, pen, and reading glasses.

She began to feel uncomfortable, wondering why he was here and asked, "you said you had some questions."

"Yes, of course, I'm sorry, I've been working round the clock the last few days, and I'm a little punchy."

To that, she snidely replied, "You can't mean you are working day and night on this case. I wouldn't think an embezzlement case would take such a priority."

"No." He hesitated, "I.....well I've been working on something else...but back to the reason I'm here. I wondered if you could tell me how much you know about Arthur Bowles."

She looked at him with a bit of shock and said, "Detective Burch, surely you understand as Mr. Bowles' attorney, I am bound by client-attorney privilege and anything..."

He interrupted her putting his hand up and said, "Yes of course I understand, I merely meant, as a long-time resident of this town, what you can tell me about him on a personal level, based on your prior relationship with him?"

"My prior relationship? I'm not sure I understand what you mean."

"Well, he has lived here for approximately twenty years and you were born and raised in this town. I see your childhood home was just three houses down the block from

Mr. Bowles and that you were friendly with him over the years. Surely you must know a lot about him."

"Yes, I have known Arthur for many years, but our friendship was casual, and I don't know very much about him. He was just a neighbor. We spent time together talking, but mostly I talked, and he listened. We both enjoyed fishing and would fish together on occasion, but that's about it."

"Well that seems reasonable, but I was under the impression you were closer than just neighbors."

"On what basis?" she demanded.

"For one, we understand he attended your college graduation at the University of Buffalo Law School a few years back." As he ended his sentence, he looked at her above the reading glasses he had been using to read from his notes. He was clearly looking for her reaction.

His last statement hit her hard, and she froze in her seat thinking, *What? Arthur attended my law school graduation? This detective has gained information while researching my background, but why?*

She sat up a little bit straighter, leaned onto her elbows on her desk, looked him straight in the eye and stated with conviction, "Why is the county Sherriff's office looking into my background? I'm an attorney representing a client accused of a crime. I am not a suspect."

He then closed his small notebook, took a deep breath and began to slowly respond, seemingly careful to choose his next words. Layton sensed he realized she was angry and decided to back off.

"Miss Virnetti, I do apologize for giving you the wrong idea here. No, you're not a suspect, but Mr. Bowles is rather, well elusive. Given you seem to be the one person in town that is closest to him, we thought you could give us some information based on your interactions with him prior to this case."

"That's hard to believe, detective. My guess is you're looking into everyone at this point, and because of my friendship with Mr. Bowles, you think I may be an accomplice. I'm merely representing Mr. Bowles. Yes, I consider myself his friend, but I can assure you there is nothing suspicious going on here. I want to know the truth, yet I have to question why you think I know something I'm not telling you and why you think I'm in a position to help you."

She stopped at that point because she realized she was letting her emotions get out of control. She had said her piece, and now she just wanted him to leave. Leave her to her work. She needed to think.

The detective then looked at her as if he too was thinking about something else and he said, "I think I have all I need at this point, so I'll let myself out. Thank you for your time, Miss Virnetti. I'll be in touch if I need anything else." Then he left her office.

She took a few deep breaths to calm herself and then went over the conversation in her mind and thought, *In the end, the detective seemed like he was reciting rehearsed lines, as if he was simply going through the motions, being polite, and what did he say?, 'I think I have all I need'. I wonder what I had said that told him anything he might need to know. I didn't reveal anything except that he made me angry, that I truly believed in Arthur's innocence and I was confused by his questions.*

The other thing he said that bothered me was that Arthur had attended my law school graduation. I'm shocked. If that's true, why didn't I know Arthur was there? He never told me he was going to attend and how did he manage to get a ticket. Each graduate was only al-

lotted a limited number of tickets, and I had given all of mine to members of my family. But the bigger question is why would the Sheriff's office even be interested in Arthur attending my graduation? Should I ask Arthur about this? Why did Arthur attend without telling me? I certainly would have been thrilled to have him there. I'd tried to think of a way to invite him, but I couldn't find a way to give him a ticket without leaving a family member out.

Looking back on the years leading up to that graduation day, Layton remembered how supportive Arthur had been. He always encouraged her to follow her dreams, and he saw in her a potential she didn't see in herself. She thought it was because he led such a simple life, and he had time to really listen to her. He didn't have a family to consume his personal time, and his job in the real estate office offered great flexibility with his schedule.

When they talked he focused on every word she said. He asked questions and gave advice in a calm way. He gave her things to think about, options to consider. In the end, he encouraged her to strive for the things that mattered to her, and he seemed to be interested in her future as if he wanted her to succeed and was proud of her. At times she felt he was like a second father to her or a close uncle and she often wondered why he didn't have a family of his own. She believed he would have been a great husband and father and never understood why he had not chosen that life for himself.

She remembered the day she told him she had been accepted to the law school. She was excited as was he, but then her excitement waned as she told him she was worried about how she would pay for it. Her parents had helped her with all the undergraduate expenses, but they were pretty tapped out after that. When she expressed this concern to Arthur, he told her not to worry about it. He was sure something would come along to work things out.

It seemed odd how calm and sure he was of this. He said, "Don't worry, Layton, the money will be there somehow, I'm sure of it. I always find in life that things that are meant to be will be taken care of just when you need it and I'm sure you are meant to be a lawyer. You have worked so hard to get to this point and now you have been accepted to law school. The financial resources will fall into place, just wait and see. I'm right about this. Enjoy the celebration of your acceptance and don't let your financial worries get in the way of that."

"Okay, Arthur. I don't know how you can be so sure about this, but I'll keep the faith." Later she was shocked to get a call from the college telling her they had filled the gap in financial aid and loans with an alumni scholarship and she couldn't wait to tell Arthur.

Chapter Fifteen

Layton sat at the conference table in her office looking at all of the information she had gathered so far about Arthur's case. There were several newspaper articles she had collected leading up to his arrest. She had printed the articles and put them in chronological order beginning two years ago. The first article read,

"Recent interest in developing property along Willard Lake in Manfield County has brought heightened excitement to area residents. As is the case with many small rural towns in the United States, Manfield County has experienced declining property values, loss of high paying jobs, and dwindling population numbers as young people leave the area after graduating high school or college.

The County has owned most of the property surrounding the Lake and is in discussions with the local real estate office, Johnson and Reed Real Estate, to consider offering lots for sale for the purpose of building both commercial and residential sections to boost tax revenues and tourism. The Lake has historically been available with public access areas for fishing, swimming, camping, and other recreational activities.

If the land were to be developed, the County is working on a plan to maintain a small percentage for continued public access, but the majority of the acreage would be sold for future development with new zoning regulations for both commercial and residential projects."

Layton thought about Willard Lake. She had enjoyed using the Lake throughout her childhood spending holidays at one of the many parks for a cook out and swimming at the beach with her family. There was a twenty-mile paved path that surrounded the lake where you could bike or walk, and there were several camping areas used for summer camps for kids of all ages.

On one of her walks with Arthur to school, she learned that he liked to fish and they agreed to meet at the lake to fish together.

"Since you like to fish Arthur, I know of a good spot where the perch really bite, but you have to get there early in the morning."

"Sounds good, Layton. Would you show me where it is sometime?"

"Sure. How about Saturday morning?" That was all it took, and from that first Saturday at the Lake, they often met at Layton's favorite spot and fished for hours.

The first article in her stack reminded her of one of the fishing excursions and how Arthur mentioned the possibility of the Lake being developed. She was home on break from college.

He started a little hesitantly, "Ah you know Layton, there has been some talk in the real estate office about the Lake."

She looked over at him and said, "What do you mean talk? You sound nervous."

"Well, I am a little because I know how much this place means to you, the good fishing and all. The talk is around possibly developing the property around the Lake for residential and commercial purposes."

She put down her pole and turned towards him to ensure she understood every word he said and slowly asked, "You aren't saying they want to sell off the land?"

"Yes, that's what they're starting to talk about. The County feels that they could take some of the land and allow people to build residences in some areas and in others businesses could build things like restaurants or maybe a hotel or bed and breakfast to bring in some tourists. That way the County would generate some much needed tax revenue."

"When you say some of the land, do you mean they could keep some of it so the public can still use it for things like fishing and swimming?"

He smiled and began to look somewhat relieved and said, "Right, they would preserve a portion of the land for public access and wildlife."

"I guess that would be alright, but I hope they don't plan to sell off too much of it. And I think they need to be careful about how the land is developed. Do you think it's a good idea, Arthur?"

"In some ways, I wish it could just stay as it is, but looking at the numbers, financially I understand why the County is proposing this. This area is economically depressed and it's not getting any better. Think about it, Layton, when you graduate from college do you plan to look for a job here?"

She considered this for a few moments and then answered, "I wish I could, but I don't see much opportunity so I guess the answer could be no. I'm just not sure."

"Well they're just starting the conversation so who knows what'll happen."

"Arthur, will you keep me posted? Since you're in real estate, you'll be a step ahead of the media on this. Maybe you'll even get involved. For you and your office it could be a boon, right?"

In response, he laughed and shook his head up and down, then said, "Yes it could be a boon as you say. I just hope if it happens it truly is a good thing and not a curse for the area. It's such a quiet, peaceful place and the lake is a large part of the charm. I'll let you."

She then flipped through more articles positively presenting the land deal being orchestrated by Johnson and Reed Real Estate. Belmont residents and legislators were all a buzz during this period banking on the robust economic future the plans presented, and many locals were investing in the various projects.

Land was surveyed, sectioned off, and zoning laws were changed to accommodate different uses for each section. There were plans for lake front condominiums, two hotels, a golf course, and strips of retail shops, restaurants, and bars. There didn't seem to be much doubt in anyone's mind that this was going to be a new era for Belmont and Manfield County.

The articles were in chronological order. She stopped to carefully read the first article when things turned from good to bad, she felt sick to her stomach.

"The Belmont Police Department is opening an investigation into the financial practices of Johnson and Reed Real Estate surrounding the Willard Lake Development Project. The investigation is in response to area resident complaints that requests to view financial records required to be made public have been delayed. Documented complaints include two residents reporting that requests for return of investment funds have been denied."

Subsequent articles noted a person of interest in the investigation had been identified, and eventually that person was named as Arthur Bowles, his arrest ensued shortly thereafter.

Chapter Sixteen

"Hey, Arthur, how are things going today?" Layton asked as she settled in at the table with Arthur for her next visit.

"Not too bad. I'm mostly bored. Not much to do here."

"I understand. I'm working on getting you out soon. Bail hearing is set for tomorrow morning so you should be released by late afternoon."

"That sounds good. And how is the case going?"

With a sigh, she replied, "Rather a slow start I'm afraid. Usually, I come out of the gate quickly, but I have to tell you, your case is unusual, but I'm up for the challenge and confident we will build you a good defense."

"I'm sorry Layton, I know I haven't been much help."

She put her hand on his and said, "It's going to be fine. Now, let's get through some things I need to talk to you about today." She emptied out her briefcase, opened her laptop for taking notes, and began.

"I ran a background check on you and found nothing they could use against you such as prior arrests, financial problems, or anything negative, so that's good. Also learned you were born to a single mother. I never knew. Can you tell me a little about your childhood?"

"Not much to tell. It was just Mom and me. We got by alright with her working in manufacturing. I never went to college, decided to get into real estate because I could take a short course and a test to get my license and begin working right away."

She looked up from her laptop and asked, "Is your mom still alive?"

"No. She died several years ago, leukemia."

"I'm sorry, Arthur. What about any other family?"

"None. Mom was raised in foster care."

"Well I guess we won't have to worry about any skeletons in the closet, will we?"

With a brief laugh he responded, "Nope, not from Arthur Bowles," then slowly repeated, "no skeletons in the closet."

"Moving on to another subject, I had a visit from a detective the other day. He wanted to ask me some questions about you, but the conversation ended pretty quickly when I emphasized the privilege of our relationship. He did mention something that surprised me though. He said you attended my law school graduation. Is that true?"

Arthur looked away without a word.

"So it is true. Why didn't you tell me?"

"I didn't want to impose on your celebration with your family, that's all."

"First of all, you wouldn't have been imposing. Remember I told you I tried to get you a ticket, but secondly, how in the hell did you get a ticket?"

"I made a small donation to the college and told them I would appreciate it if I could get just one ticket and they were happy to oblige."

"A small donation? How much?"

"Enough to get a ticket, but I didn't want you to know, so I just went, sat in the back and left before you met up with your parents."

"Alright Arthur, I think we can leave it at that for now, but I wish you had told me and joined us."

"I'm sorry, Layton. At the time I thought I was doing the right thing."

"It's okay. Now, let's move on to something more relevant to your case. I have some disclosure documents related to the evidence they have. Seems the most damning is financial transactions. You've got some funds moving around that I don't understand so maybe we can go through it, and you can enlighten me."

Over the next couple hours, Layton went over Arthur's financial records including statements from his current bank account and the transactions for the period of time in question, mainly since the land deal started. She explained that one of the reasons he was accused of embezzlement was that bank records showed several transactions with thousands of dollars each moved to an offshore account. At this Arthur became agitated.

"I don't have an offshore account. Something is wrong here." He grabbed the bank statement. "The only money I moved out of my account was moved to the holding account for the investors, and it was rare that I received any funds into my personal account."

"Really? Well, it's all right here in black and white. It looks like there was a lot of money coming into your account then moved to that offshore account in your name."

He stood up, ran his hand through his hair and said, "I tell you, these are not right. I never opened any account offshore and look," he said as he picked up one of his personal bank statements, "there's way too much money going into this account. At the beginning of the project, people were excited and wanted to get in on this investment opportunity, so they were writing checks out to me. I gave them receipts and opened a separate account as soon as I could get a shell corporation established. I moved everything related to the land deal to that account."

"Didn't you see this before?"

"No, I wasn't looking at the statements that closely. Everything happened so fast and quite frankly, this whole deal was way over our heads at the real estate office."

He then took all of the statements and started reviewing them more closely. After several minutes, he continued, "Look, Layton. When this started I can see deposits that are reasonable, and you can see they were moved out, that's when I transferred investors' money to the shell corporation's account. Then after that, there are no significant deposits because I put money directly into the investor account and I wouldn't even accept checks written out to me personally. Now, look here, just over the past few months I see funds coming in again and moved out the same day. Are those the ones going to the off shore account?"

She reviewed her records and said, "Yes, that lines up, and you say you did not execute those moves during these recent months?"

"No," he stated, "I did NOT."

"And you don't remember setting up the offshore account?"

"I am absolutely sure I did not open that account!" Arthur was hot, and she could see he was telling the truth.

"You say when investors gave you money, and you put it into your personal account in the beginning, you gave them receipts."

"Yes, I gave them a receipt," he continued as he pounded the table with his finger, emphasizing each word. "EVERY SINGLE TIME."

"Now this is very important, Arthur. Do you have copies of those receipts and if so, where are they?"

"They're in the real estate office, but since the funds went into my personal account, I also made copies for myself, and I have them at home so I could use them to reconcile my account."

"Beautiful! After you're released, I'm going to need you to give me those copies."

The next day Arthur's bail hearing resulted in his release from jail. He was able to return to work, but because he was accused of embezzlement of funds surrounding a land development deal in the local community, it was decided best that he take a leave of absence until the trial was over. Arthur went home, and Layton returned to her office and got back to work on the case.

She decided to look into Arthur's donation to her law school and his obtaining a ticket to graduation. She wasn't entirely sure why, thinking it didn't matter much to his case, but she was curious.

"Business Office. How can I help you?"

"Hello, this is Attorney Layton Virnetti. I'm a graduate of the law school and currently working on a case. I was hoping you could help me with something."

"I sure will if I can Ms. Virnetti. Whatcha need?"

"When I attended, my financial aid had quite a gap that was quickly filled by what I was told was some sort of alumni scholarship. Can you give me any specific information about that scholarship?"

"Let me look you up." After Layton provided the necessary information such as dates of attendance, social security number, and full name, the woman on the phone said, "Here we go. I see all of your grants and loans .... then oh, yes, here it is. No, doesn't look like the typical alumni scholarship from the general fund, looks like it came from a restricted fund."

"Restricted fund? What exactly does that mean?" Layton asked.

"It was set up through funds from an anonymous donor. That isn't very common, but it does happen. So a person wants to help pay for a student's college but doesn't want the person to know who they are so they donate to the college and the funds are only to be used for a specific person's expenses. We set it up in a restricted fund."

"And that's how my gap was filled?"

"Yes, for the entire time you were attending. Then any funds remaining are to be transferred to our general alumni scholarship fund, provided the donor is in agreement of course. I see there wasn't a big amount left, but there was a small transfer after you graduated."

"Can you tell me who the donor was? It could be important to the client I am currently defending."

"Oh, no, I couldn't possibly do that."

"I understand. Thank you for your help." Layton hung up the phone and quickly dialed the college again, this time asking for the Bursar's Office. As she often did when looking for information, she pretended to be an accountant working for a client -

"Hello, this is Rebecca Davis with the Davis CPA firm. I have a client who is being audited, and one of the issues relates to funds he donated to the college. I need to confirm the amount of excess funds that would have been kept and moved to the general alumni scholarship fund. He designated his donations to one student several years ago."

"I can help you with that. What was the name of the student and the years of attendance?" After Layton provided the information, the gentleman on the phone replied, "Here it is. After the funds were used for Ms. Virnetti's expenses, $1,357 was transferred to the general fund. We then would have issued a statement to the donor with that information."

"Can you verify where the statement was sent? My client doesn't seem to have received it, and we wondered if the address was correct."

"Sure. To Mr. Arthur Bowles at ....."

Chapter Seventeen

Layton took another cookie and poured more tea for herself and Hank.

"Like I said, Dad, I have my ways, and I'll get what I need. Over the past few weeks, since I started his case, I've been doing what I can to get information since he's not helping much."

"Lucky for Arthur."

"Hope you're right. I have a stop to make on my way home to do just that."

Layton pulled into a parking lot on fifth, an out-of-date strip mall where several businesses were located some having been there for many years. There was a barber shop, nail salon, liquor store, convenience store, and a pawn shop. She entered the pawn shop and was immediately welcomed by the owner sitting behind the counter.

"Hey, Layton. Where the hell you been?" He was big around and tall with a long beard. He wore an American flag bandana around his head and a leather vest over a white t-shirt. The vest displayed a patch that read *Vietnam Vet and Proud*. She walked behind the counter and gave him a big hug.

"I've been busy working on a case, but I've missed you, Ronnie."

"Yup, I read about it in the papers. That big land deal around the lake gone bad, right?"

"Right. My client is Arthur Bowles. You remember him, don't you? I brought him in once, and he bought a few things."

Ronnie shook his head up and down and said, "Sure do. Seemed like a real nice dude, kinda quiet, but real nice. Do you think he's innocent?"

"I'm sure of it. I've known him for a long time, and this just isn't something he would do. He's not the type to swindle anyone. He lives so modestly that I can't picture him needing all that money for anything."

"Well, if you believe in him, I believe in him. You always seem to know about people. Hell, you see through my exterior into the real man," he stated, as he patted his belly and pulled on his beard and laughed. "So what you need from me, sweetie?"

"I need you to do some digging for me. I need information about something that's puzzling to both Arthur and me."

Layton visited Ronnie periodically when working on a case because he was not just the owner of a pawn shop, he was an expert on the computer. They went into his back room where he worked his magic on the web.

"Wow, Ronnie, you've been adding equipment since the last time I stopped by."

"Oh just tinkerin' with stuff people drop off. Been doing a little repair and virus protection work on the side. Seems once you know how to hack around, you get real good at keeping the bad guys out, but the crooks're getting better and better all the time."

"That's why I need your help." She went on to explain how Arthur's bank transactions were suspect with things coming and going that he couldn't explain. "So I need you to see if you can find any trail that leads to who could be setting some things up in Arthur's name without his knowledge. We both believe he is being framed, but at this point, it looks like he took the money and moved it off shore. He swears he never opened any offshore account."

"Okay. Give me all the details you have, and I'll get to work. Now remember what I find has to stay between us, not used as evidence, but might give you some answers."

She lifted her hand, "I know, I know. Like you always say, you have to go in the back door instead of the front and sometimes it's necessary to jimmy the lock."

The following Monday when Layton arrived at her office she was surprised to see Detective Burch parked in front of her building. As she entered, he got out of the car and followed her in.

"Detective Burch," she said as he opened the door for her, "what is it now?"

"Ms. Virnetti."

"Please, call me Layton."

"Alright, Layton. I wanted to stop by to let you know I think we got off on the wrong foot the other day. I never meant to imply that you were a suspect."

"Okay, but it sure seemed that way. So how can I help you today because again I must emphasize my attorney client privilege..."

He interrupted her as they entered her office, "I understand, and I'm sorry I gave you the wrong impression. We're working on this case too."

"Wait, why? You've arrested Arthur and turned the case over to the District Attorney. Your work should be done."

"Yes, I know, but we still want to make sure we have the right man, and the Sheriff has me working in an unofficial capacity until the trial." At this point, he paused and stared as if waiting for her reaction. She gave none, so he continued. "There seems to be enough evidence to charge Arthur, but we've been puzzled by motive. Greed is always a good one, yet in Arthur's case, it doesn't fit."

With caution, she replied, "Go on."

"Arthur's pretty clean, and the way he lives just doesn't match the profile of a swindler. Usually, they live higher than their income and have a lot of debt. Sometimes they gamble, get in trouble with the wrong people, you know what I'm saying, right?"

Again she proceeded with caution, "Yes, I know what you're saying."

"These types usually commit the crime, especially the first one, because they're up against the wall and have to do something to get out from under."

"You're right. In this case, things don't fit and having known Arthur for as long as I have I'm sure he is not motivated by greed, but again I ask what do you want from me?"

"I just wanted to stop by and apologize for the other day and let you know I have my doubts as well and want to get to the truth. If we can help each other accomplish that, I'm willing to work together - within the parameters of the law of course. I can see that you want to get to the truth and you're not in this just to defend your client."

She softened and said, "Detective Burch, you have just learned something about me that hits right to my core. I only defend clients that I believe are innocent and that will never change for me. Can I get you some coffee?"

"Yes, I would like that if you have the time to continue our conversation."

As she made them each a cup of coffee she continued, "You're right about Arthur being clean. There's not much at all in his background, not even a speeding ticket. And he won't tell me much. You probably know more about him than I do having done the investigation before he was charged. It's been tough determining a strategy for his defense."

They drank their coffee and talked for a few more minutes, and the Detective assured her he would let her know if there was anything that developed that he could share. She, however, knew that she would not be sharing much with him. She would have her guard up and would protect Arthur, trust no one, not even a detective from the Sheriff's office.

Hank sat in his easy chair in the den with an after dinner drink waiting for Layton's mom to finish cleaning up the kitchen. She would join him soon. He gazed out the window at the woods that lined their backyard. His thoughts were focused on his daughter and the case she was working on for Arthur. He knew this was going to be difficult and oh how he wished he could help, but what could he do? Nothing."

"Hey, Hon. Layton's on the phone," his wife called from the kitchen. He picked up the extension in the den and said, "Hi Honey. What's up? How is Ronnie?"

"What? How'd you know I've been to see Ronnie?"

"Lucky guess. Last time we talked you said you have ways and I know Ronnie is one of your ways. So how is he? I haven't seen him in a while."

"He's doing pretty good."

"Can he help with this one?"

"Of course he can, or at least I hope he can. I really need it. But, that's not why I called. I was wondering if you would mind giving me some help in the office, maybe on Saturdays. I'm getting pretty busy, but not busy enough to hire any help. You always seem interested in my cases, so I was thinking you could help me with Arthur's case. I ran it by him first, and he's fine with it."

Hank bit his lip. He was not surprised but thought this might put him in an awkward position, however, his baby girl was asking for his help. How could he refuse?"

"Dad? You still there?"

"Yeah, just thinking, I may have to work some overtime soon. We're getting busy at the plant, but I'm sure that'll only be Saturday mornings. I could come in after that if you buy me lunch."

"Of course I'll buy us lunch. We'll eat, then get right to work."

"How do you think I can help?"

"Oh just organize things. I know this one's going to take a big chunk of my time and I'll be tempted to let it consume me. I have to make sure I devote ample time to my other cases. Arthur's case is also more difficult so we can go through everything I find and that Ronnie comes up with and put our heads together to build the best case."

"Okay. That sounds good. I'll do what I can, but I'm no lawyer."

"Dad, you've always been there for me to bounce things off of. You have a knack for the legal stuff. If I fill you in on all the evidence and info I have, you'll be even more help to me. Can we start this weekend?"

"Sure, honey. This Saturday works for me. I'll let you know if I have to work in the morning and what time I can be there. Either way, you owe me lunch."

After he hung up, his wife came in and took his empty glass. She made him another drink and joined him with one for herself. He smiled at her in appreciation. He needed it, but couldn't tell her why.

Chapter Eighteen

"Detective Burch thank you for seeing me. How are things going with the case? Any progress with Ms. Virnetti?"

"Some progress through my conversations with her. I can tell you she was surprised to learn Arthur attended her graduation from law school."

"Did she say that?" asked the man sitting across from the detective.

"No not specifically, but her reaction gave it away, then she quickly tried to hide her feelings. She was pretty angry with me for asking her about her relationship with Arthur."

"Too much too fast, huh?"

Detective Burch shook his head in agreement and continued, "That's right, so I backed off quickly in our first meeting. After that, I changed my approach making her think I wanted us to help each other. Told her I wanted to get the truth just as much as she did and if there was anything I could tell her I would."

"Do you think Arthur is being straight with me about how much he has told her?" the man asked.

"Oh yeah. She has no idea. As a matter of fact, she's been ticked at him for not telling her much about his past, but then she did some thorough background work on him and found there's not much for him to tell."

The man was silent for a few minutes, deep in thought. The detective looked out the window and drank from his coffee cup waiting for the next question.

"What are your thoughts about the case? Do you think she'll be able to get him off?" the man asked.

"At this point, my guess is as good as yours. If I was a bettin' man I would say she may not be able to no matter how good she is and let me tell you, she's good. There's a lot of evidence against him which surprises me."

The other man frowned. "I have to agree with you. You know most of the guys are dirty, but this one I'm sure stays within the law. Do you think someone could be framing him?"

"Possibly," the detective answered.

"Oh great! This is just what we need."

"Well, if someone is setting him up, we have to hope Layton can find out who that is, prove it, and then get him through the trial and out of this mess." The detective added, "We know there are people out there that would love to get revenge."

"Right, but I thought we had him fully protected. Now, this makes me think there might be a leak somewhere and someone knows something."

The detective lifted both hands with palms down and motioned up and down as he said, "Just dial back a bit - give it some time. We don't know what's what yet. If someone is framing him, it might not be what you fear, and this could all end well. "

The man sighed and said, "I know, you're right Burch. I've thought about that. It's just that I've been so involved in this one and I hate to have to make a change." The man rose and headed towards the door then turned and said, "Thanks for the update. I'll be in touch. Keep doing what you're doing with as much subtlety as possible."

Chapter Nineteen

Arthur was late for his appointment at Layton's office, but it couldn't be helped. After he made his apologies, they sat at a table in her conference room, and she went through her usual routine spreading out documents that she wanted to go over and opened her laptop for note taking.

She was about to begin with her list, then slowly pushed things aside, clasped her hand together in front of her and said, "Arthur, I have to ask you something."

"Go ahead."

"Why did you pay for my law school gap in funding?"

"How did you find that out? It was intended to remain confidential." He seemed irritated.

"I know, but I'm good at investigating and how I found out isn't important, what is important is why."

"Why is not important. I did it because you needed it. Period."

As the conversation continued he became more irritated and the more irritated he became, the more focused and calm Layton appeared.

"That was incredibly generous and thoughtful of you, and before I go on, I need to thank you for that. I don't know what I would have done if the funding you provided hadn't come through for me."

Arthur looked away, intent on not letting her look into his eyes as he spoke. "You're welcome. I was happy to do it, that's all. It wasn't that much, and it's not like I have a family to support or kids to put through college like your parents did."

She grabbed his hands in hers and softly said, "That meant so much to me, and I don't know how I would be where I am today without your help with support and financial assistance - so again - thank you."

The phone rang interrupting their tender moment, much to Arthur's satisfaction having been made to feel uncomfortable by the whole conversation.

She answered, "Layton Virnetti."

"Layton, it's Ronnie. Is this a good time?"

"Yes, Ronnie. I have Arthur here with me now. What've you got for me?" Arthur could only hear one side of the conversation, but Layton seemed pleased and excited by what Ronnie had to tell her.

When she hung up, Arthur said, "What was that about?"

"Pay dirt!" she exclaimed as she clapped her hands together and jumped out of her chair. "This is beautiful, Arthur, be-a-u-ti-ful."

"Layton, come on, tell me what's going on. Who is Ronnie?"

"Okay," she said as she sat back in the chair, "Ronnie is a guy who gets information for me that I can't get from anyone else. You met him once. He owns the pawn shop on fifth."

"Oh right, I remember him."

"He's sort of a wiz on the computer, mostly dark web and boy did he come through for me this time."

Arthur's head dropped, and he looked up at her with raised eyebrows and said, "You mean he's a hacker. Comes by this information illegally?"

"Not completely. Sometimes he calls in favors, but most of what he finds, we can't use as evidence, just gets us on the right track."

"Are you sure we should be doing things this way. I mean, I don't like illegal methods."

"Yes, Arthur, I know you don't. Hell, that's one of the reasons I'm so sure of your innocence, but after what you told me about the bank accounts, I also know someone is out there playing dirty pool, and we can't afford to do everything by the book."

"What do you mean, why not?"

"Think about it this way. When a person commits a crime, they hide things, bury evidence, the trail of evidence isn't transparent. Their methods are not legal, so sometimes in order to find that evidence and defend a client, I have to use unconventional means."

"Unconventional, huh? I can think of a few other words to describe it, and I don't like it."

She responded, "Let me tell you a little about Ronnie. He served in the Army during the Vietnam War. He was involved in military intelligence within the Army Security Agency or ASA, and their work involved monitoring North Vietnamese radio traffic, safeguarding the Army's signal system and obtaining information needed for tactical and planning purposes to help with fighting the war. Ronnie was just seventeen years old when he volunteered. The work he did during the war was important, and the work he does now is done for honorable reasons. Arthur, he's one of the good guys, but sometimes you have to use methods to uncover the truth and get justice for the innocent that you or I may not be comfortable with. You could say his methods are justified by the result. You could call it *justifiable deception.*"

Arthur paused in thought. She waited patiently for him to consider all she had said. He then said, "I suppose I understand. If it has to be done to prove my innocence, I'll accept your methods ... with some reluctance."

Layton then went on to explain what Ronnie had uncovered.

Chapter Twenty

After their meeting in Layton's office, Arthur returned home. Sitting in a comfortable leather chair in his den he ate a sandwich for dinner followed up by a stiff drink. His thoughts returned to something she said during their conversation.

Justified by the result. I understand that very well. Better than Layton will ever know. If I could go back and undo what I've done, the choices I've made, would I do things differently? Would Layton see my choices as justified? I wonder. She's always been so grounded in her views, so sure of herself. Will she ever waiver, question her beliefs as I've been forced to do? I do believe circumstances can lead to alterations in our way of thinking about things. She would probably experience this if she knew the truth about me.

He finished his drink and poured another. From his wallet, he withdrew a piece of paper that when unfolded revealed a single phone number. He dialed the number, and after a man answered, he said, "It's Arthur. I need to talk."

"Okay. Now or do we need to meet?"

"Now is fine. Just came from a meeting with my lawyer. She's uncovered something that could be helpful to my case and needs me to do some digging at the real estate office."

"That's good. Can you do it?"

"I don't know. I'm sort of suspended because of the bad publicity, but it seemed a little unreasonable. I could be in the office working on clerical stuff until the trial is over. I don't have to be in the field selling or exposed to the public."

The man asked, "What does she suspect is going on?"

"Someone in the office is trying to frame me."

"Ah, how did she learn that?"

"I'd rather not say, but now she needs me to find some evidence to support it. I have an idea about how to do it, and it's partly based on the truth. I'm bored out of my mind sitting at home, so I'm going to go to see the owner, Justin Johnson and plead with him to let me come back to work. I'll emphasize my willingness to stay out-of-sight, just doing paperwork and maybe even working in the evening part of the time when things in town are quiet. That will give me a chance to work alone."

"Sounds good, Arthur. Keep me informed on your progress." Arthur hung up the phone and finished his drink. He would go to the office the next morning.

As he entered the office, he smiled at Justin and said, "Good morning! How are things going in the real estate business?"

"Arthur," he sounded surprised. "Not bad. What are you doing here?"

"I just wanted to stop by and say hello, see how you were making out with all that's going on. Oh, who am I kidding? Justin, I'm going crazy being away with nothing to do day after day. I thought maybe it was premature to ask me to take time off."

"Sit down Arthur," Justin said as he pulled out a chair. "You know we can't have you selling right now. People believe you swindled them out of their money for God's sake."

"I know that, but isn't there something I could do around the office? I'd be willing to make coffee, empty waste baskets, do filing, anything at all. Just let me be here doing something." Arthur pleaded with as much sincerity as he could display.

With some hesitation, Justin replied, "That would be alright, but people would still see you coming into and leaving the office on a regular basis. I just don't think it would look right."

"I thought of that so how about this. I could come in later in the afternoon and work into the evening or maybe on weekends. Don't you think it would be better to demonstrate that you believe in my innocence instead of acting as if you have already judged me guilty?" Arthur looked him in the eye and wouldn't look away until he gave an answer. He could sense he was making a good case and getting through to Justin.

"I suppose you have a point. Of course, I don't believe you're guilty, but there's a lot of evidence to the contrary. Let's have you come in as you said towards the end of the day and we'll see what we can have you work on. I have just one condition, if negative rumblings start around town and I feel it's hurting the business in any way, we'll have to stop, deal?"

Arthur stood and offered his hand to Justin saying, "Deal and thanks. This means a lot to me, and we'll see how it goes. Remember anything you want me to do, let me know. I merely want to do something to keep my mind off this whole thing and keep me busy."

For the next few weeks, Layton worked on reviewing the evidence in Arthur's case, lining up local witnesses, writing her opening statement for trial, and meeting with Arthur. Finding the witnesses presented the biggest challenge because so many locals had invested in the project and even if they didn't invest, they knew someone who did. Her star character witness was Charles Winton, the owner of the only hardware store in town.

She thought of him as a witness for Arthur when she remembered an incident that happened one day at the Hardware store. She was there buying some paint supplies for her father and Arthur was picking up paint for the real estate office. They were working on painting the façade to make it look better now that they were getting a lot of attention surrounding the development project and the owner felt the place needed to be spruced up.

As they both stood at the counter, they could hear the owner of the hardware store, Charles, spouting off in the office about some letter he had just received in the mail. It was unusual for Charles to speak of business matters so that customers could hear, but he was clearly distraught, and she guessed he couldn't help but raise his voice so that anyone in the store, including Arthur, could hear.

After a couple of minutes trying to ignore this, Arthur went into the office to see what was going on. He left the door open, and Layton heard him say, "Charles, what's happened?"

Charles replied, "Oh the crazy State says I owe back sales tax and I'm sure I paid everything I owe. I always do. I don't mess around with taxes because I know too many businesses that have to close if they don't do things right and the State catches up with them."

She could see Charles hand the letter to Arthur, he quickly skimmed it and handed it back. Then he patted Charles on the back and said a few words. Charles looked relieved and shook Arthur's hand, folded the letter, put it back in the envelope and set it on his desk. Arthur came out of the office and joined her at the counter.

After both paid for their purchases, they left the store together and once outside, Layton asked, "That was intense, Arthur, what was it all about?"

He explained that Charles received a letter about not paying his sales tax and Arthur assured him if he paid them and had copies of the sales tax return or confirmation that he filed on-line with a receipt or cancelled check, there would be no problem. Arthur said he would stop by tomorrow and help him contact the State to straighten it out.

At the time she thought it was great that Arthur was able to help, but recently wondered why he knew how to help so quickly and confidently. He was a real estate agent, and through her research into his background, she learned he never went to college nor did he ever own a business.

At this point, however, it didn't matter. Charles was a strong supporter of Arthur and, most incredibly, Charles was an investor. He didn't lose as much as some, but still, he lost and ironically believed in Arthur's innocence. He would make a credible witness.

Arthur spent as much time as possible in the office without drawing suspicion from Justin working through assignments Justin gave him before leaving for the day. Then when alone in the office at night, Arthur searched for answers.

Ronnie had found that the offshore account lead back to Justin. It wasn't a clear path as it wound its way through multiple shell corporations in a few different banks in various countries, but the funds ultimately ended up accessible to Justin Johnson. Arthur's task was to find something to prove it. At one point he decided he needed help.

"Ron's Pawn Shop."

"Hello, is this Ronnie?"

"Sure is, what can I do ya for?"

"This is Arthur Bowles."

"Hey, Arthur! How's it going?"

"Not too bad, but I'm trying to find something concrete to connect Johnson to that offshore account that Layton can use, and I'm stuck. I can't believe I'm asking this, but is there any way you can get me into Justin's computer at the office. He usually brings his laptop home at night, but he left it here, and it's an opportunity I hate to pass up. He went golfing this afternoon, and I guess he wasn't planning on doing any work at home after that."

"Well you're in luck then aren'cha? Sure I might be able to do that. Give me his IP address, and I'll get to work on it."

Within the hour Ronnie was in, and Arthur went to work. Fortunately, his efforts were fruitful, and he couldn't wait to fill Layton in.

Layton and Hank cleaned up the conference room table after having lunch together in her office. As promised, Hank showed up promptly at 12:30 after work Saturday afternoon and, as Layton had promised, lunch was delivered and ready when he arrived.

"Had enough, Dad?"

"Yup. I'm fat and happy and ready to work."

"Hopefully you're not too satisfied, ready for a nap."

"Maybe, I could use another cup of coffee."

"Okay, here you go." Layton proceeded to pour them both another cup of coffee, then she brought over a file box and spread its contents on the table.

"What are we working on today?" her father asked.

"Today we're going through every piece of information and evidence I have from the beginning, including the arrest warrant, newspaper articles, Arthur's statement to the police, the background check I did on Arthur..."

"Background check? You did a background check on your client?"

"Yup. Had to. You know how damn private Arthur is. I couldn't get much out of him about his past, so I had to do my own checking."

At which point she dug through the pile, and after finding the printed file, threw it across the table to Hank. He flipped through the pages.

"Not much here is there?"

"No, but in a way that's good, no criminal record. I can use that in his defense."

Once everything was out of the box, Layton and Hank spent the next hour sorting things into categories. Evidence presented to her as part of the discovery process before trial, documents Arthur provided from his own records, information she collected from newspaper articles, background checks, and interviews with Arthur and character witnesses. It was boring work, but Hank seemed to be interested in how she was approaching this case.

"How are things going with Ronnie? Has he been able to help in any way?"

"He's helping set us in the right direction."

"If there's one thing I know, Layton, if anyone can get the goods, Ronnie can."

"So, Dad, how did you meet Ronnie?"

"I guess I met him at the pawn shop. I've known him for years. When your mom and I were first married, we didn't have much, and one Christmas I wanted to get her a nice piece of jewelry. The pawn shop seemed like a good place to start. I thought an antique ring or necklace would be good, and Ronnie had some pretty solid stuff from estate sales."

"I never knew that. Which piece of jewelry did you get?"

"You know the ring she wears on her right hand with the diamond surrounded by rubies? That's the one."

"From the pawn shop? Was she okay with that?"

"Definitely. It's a beautiful ring, and we would never have been able to afford anything close to that on our budget. She was thrilled when I gave it to her."

"That's cool, Dad."

"And I've been friends with Ronnie ever since. I have him work on our computers too."

"Putting me on to him for some investigative work with my cases was the best tip you've ever given me. You know, I have to say, I'm sort of enjoying these Saturday work sessions."

"Me too," Hank replied with a smile.

After Hank left the office, Layton checked her email and found a message from Arthur letting her know he wanted to meet, that he had some information for her. They agreed to meet in her office the next day at two o'clock.

Chapter Twenty One

When Arthur entered her office, he was holding a stack of papers. As he slapped them down on her desk, he smiled and said, "Pay dirt!"

"Really? What have you got?"

"I found it right on his computer. He's going to regret that golf game."

"What golf game?"

"Never mind. Not important, but Justin's laptop was in the office, and I was alone, so I asked Ronnie to help me hack into it and..."

"What, you the highly ethical Arthur Bowles lowering yourself to hacking?"

"Very funny, Layton. I realized that if I'm not the one who committed the crime, I should be justified in this method of research if I uncover the real criminal."

"Uhuh. So what did you find?"

"It's all right here in black and white. He created three shell corporations and funneled money through them with wire transfers. He kept a record for himself of all the transactions and moves. Look – here's where most of the investors' funds are, accounts that snake back to him and his wife, so she's in on it too ... I think. The funds in the account offshore in my name are only a portion of the total, and that must be what he did so he could frame me if this went south before they left the country."

"What do you mean before they left the country?"

"That's the best part! I found their travel plans and the date of departure was to occur shortly after this whole thing went down and embezzlement was suspected. They almost made it."

"This is good stuff. Now we need to take it all in and come up with our plan of action."

"What do you mean? Just take it to the DA and get the charges against me dropped!" Arthur replied with excitement.

"No, we can't do that. First of all, you had Ronnie hack into Justin's computer. Secondly, you still have funds in an offshore account in your name. Thirdly Justin just let you back into the office to work. See where I'm going here?"

"Yes, I do. I would still be a suspect. Does this mean you can't use this pile of documents as evidence?"

"It's not all that bad. The DA could keep you as a suspect building their case on your collusion with Justin to embezzle investors' money, but there are ways to use this evidence. My first thought is that you could testify that Justin left his computer unlocked when he left for the day, and you innocently stumbled on the information. We can even ask Ronnie to make it look that way, but I don't think we will go that route."

"So what do you think we should do with this information?"

Layton tapped her fingers on the pile of papers on the desk, bit her lip then said slowly, "We have a few options. We could let Justin know we have something incriminating." She stood up and began pacing. "We could give it to the DA, but they'd just throw it back at me because I can't say how we obtained it. Sit tight for now, and we'll get together again to discuss things."

"Sounds good, but you think we're going to be able to use this to get me off right?"

"Yes, Arthur, the most important thing is we now know Justin is the embezzler and he's framing you. Here's the proof. It's my job to figure out how to use it. Great work!"

Arthur went through all the events in his mind of the past couple of years leading up to his arrest. He had been working day after day in the real estate office listing and showing property, some residential, some commercial. Each day was pretty slow and easy without much excitement. He didn't mind. His life was uncomplicated, and he made enough money to support his lifestyle and had no complaints. The owner of the office, however, was not satisfied with the sales levels. Justin Johnson had inherited the business from his grandfather, Harold.

Harold Johnson had started the business many years before with his fiancé Joyce Reed, and the two of them handled all facets of the office. They enjoyed building the business in their community and raising a family but never wanted the business to grow to the point that required adding additional staff or space. They chose not to carry any debt on the business and hoped one day they could hand the business down to a family member. Justin began working in the office during college and became the obvious choice as the one to carry on the business.

Justin worked alongside his grandfather until Harold retired and up until both of his grandparents passed away, he stuck to the vision of remaining small earning a decent living. When Arthur began working in the office, he was encouraged by the fact that the company was small in a quiet town with expectations on the low side for selling agents. He wasn't looking for a competitive environment, and he was happy with a modest income, and he enjoyed working that way for several years. Then about six months after Harold's death, things started to change, and he sensed Justin was about to shift strategies for his business. The agents were called into Justin's office for an early morning meeting.

"Thanks guys for coming in early today. I have some news for you that could impact our business in a big way. I wanted to start today by filling you in on this new opportunity and also, to begin planning our strategy." Arthur shifted uncomfortably in his seat as Justin continued, "A buddy of mine sits on the town council, and he has been in contact with a woman he went to college with. Apparently, she came home with him one year for spring break, and they spent a lot of time at the lake. She was studying to be an architect and now works for an architectural/construction firm that specializes in prime property development. She never forgot our little lake and its potential, and now her firm would like to pursue a major project to develop lakefront and surrounding property."

That was how it all began. After the meeting with the three agents, Justin asked Arthur to stay and to close the door to his office.

Arthur sat back down, and Justin continued, "Arthur, I know you haven't been here long, but you're the best agent I have. It's not that you crush it on the selling side, but you have a nice way with people, and I can tell you have a good business sense. I want you to head this up."

"What do you mean? Is there something more going on?"

"Yes. I didn't want to divulge too much, but my buddy says he can clear the way for this office to be the lead agent and broker for any deals related to the development project. We can get in on this right at the start, and I need someone like you to be the one to keep us organized. I've seen your organizational skills, your attention to detail. Your paperwork is impeccable."

"Sure, I can handle that, I guess, but won't the others feel slighted? I know I've been here for a number of years, but I was the last one hired, and the other agents do sell more than I do."

"Doesn't matter. You're the man I want for the job. I know you'll take it seriously and I can count on you. You're honest and full of integrity. I feel people in this community will trust you."

"Trust me? Why do they need to trust me?"

Justin came around to the front of his desk and put a hand on Arthur's shoulder which made Arthur slightly uncomfortable.

"Arthur, don't you get it? We'll be putting out several opportunities for locals to invest in this project. Sure there'll be others from outside the area, but in these cases, you need the community to support it and one of the ways to ensure that support is to offer them a piece of the action." He then slapped Arthur on the back and returned to his seat and asked, "Can I count on you?"

Arthur hesitantly replied, "Yes, you can count on me. I'll do what you ask, manage the administrative side of the project."

As he thought through that first meeting, he realized Justin may have been setting him up as the scapegoat right from the start. It was all beginning to make sense. Arthur was trustworthy, and even though people didn't know him well on a personal level, he had a solid reputation from his years selling real estate. Folks were always happy with the transactions he brokered because he wasn't motivated by commissions alone and cared about helping people get what they wanted with a fair deal.

There were times when Arthur felt uncomfortable as Justin seemed to push more and more responsibility his way on this project. Arthur now believed the investor deposits that ended up in Arthur's account clearly had a purpose and they were part of the frame up. Justin was brighter than Arthur ever gave him credit for. He played Arthur. Now Arthur wanted to nail the bastard and hoped Layton would find a way to do it.

Chapter Twenty Two

Layton entered the restaurant scanning the booths, looking for Detective Burch. He was sitting toward the back, and she noted the obvious, no one was sitting in any adjourning booths.

"Detective Burch," she said as she joined him in the booth. "Thank you for seeing me."

"Of course, Layton, anytime. You said you have some information for me?"

"Yes, I do, but first I have to tell you it's not exactly something that can be used in court."

He laughed and said, "Ninety percent of what I get falls into that category so don't worry, we can use whatever you've got in some way or another. Go on."

"I believe Justin Johnson, the owner of the real estate firm, is the one you need to investigate. It seems he is trying to frame Arthur."

"How sure are you and why?"

She pulled out a few pages from her bag and put them on the table.

"This documents a trail of transactions on Justin's computer proving he set up an off shore account in Arthur's name and then moved funds to it from the shell corporation Arthur set up to temporarily hold the investors' initial contributions to the project. In addition, Justin and his wife were planning to leave the country right around the time the local Police began the investigation and temporarily halted travel plans for anyone connected to the project. You can check airline records and get that information yourself."

"And can I ask how you came to hold this documentation?"

She sat back and said with a sly smile, "Sure you can ask, but I'm not going to tell you."

"I could've guessed that, but it was worth a shot. This is helpful anyway. I'll let you in on something that's been happening. We've been pressuring the people in the district attorney's office to look into other suspects. This will help us to *encourage* them to get a search warrant for Justin's office. They have grounds since the deal involves one of their agents."

"I know so why haven't they done it up until now?"

"They like easy cases, probably because they have too many to handle. You know the story. Too many cases, too few attorneys with heavy workloads and don't even get me started on how little they get paid. Public servants you know."

"But still, they should be more thorough."

"So far everything has led to Arthur. They follow the evidence, and it was all there. Easy pickin's!"

"Sure, until you consider motive and first time offense and...."

"I hear ya, Layton, but that's a lawyer's defense approach. Law enforcement and prosecution come from a different angle. Now, this information changes things. It's something that explains some of the evidence against Arthur, and I think we'll be able to find a strong motive for Justin if we start looking."

"So you might be able to use this to get the DA to push for a search warrant for Justin's office, his computer, and specifically his bank records as well."

"Should be able to. Let us take it from here."

"Sounds good to me. Detective Burch, can I ask you one last question?"

"Shoot."

"Why do you think Justin was so sloppy? I mean, I sure am glad he had stuff on his computer for Arthur to find, but it seems like a dumb move to me for a criminal."

"That's just it. He's not the criminal type, just greedy. He figured out a way to steal, set someone up and take off, but he didn't know what he was doing to cover it up completely. I have to say, however, if it wasn't for you and …. well, let's just say your methods of investigation, he might have gotten away with it."

"I'm glad you sound confident, but we still have a long way to go. Hopefully, Justin doesn't get wise and scrub the trail before the DA finds what I found."

"Try to relax, and let this play out. We're on the right track and we both want the same thing – finding the truth and convicting the right man for the crime."

Three days later Arthur went to work in the real estate office as usual at 4 pm. Justin was there working in his office, and Arthur was posting some new listings on the multiple listing site, making copies, and doing some filing when three men entered the front door. The first man asked if Justin was in. Arthur motioned to the inner office and followed the man in. He witnessed the man pulling a tri-folded document from his inner suit pocket.

He placed it on Justin's desk and stated, "We're serving you this search warrant to review records in your office, both hard copy and on all computers. We have agents at your home at this time and another agent stationed at your vehicle and will need you to open the vehicle and trunk."

"Layton, where are you?" Arthur said when she picked up her cell phone.

"In the office, why?"

"I'll be right over. You won't believe what is going down in our office at this very moment." Arthur raced over to Layton's office and blew through the door clearly out of breath.

"Arthur, what's going on?" Layton asked.

"They're there now in Justin's office with a search warrant for everything. It's happening. Finally, they suspect him. I don't know what you did, but whatever it was, it got something going." Layton jumped up from her chair and moved around to the front of her desk.

"Yes! It worked. I gave the information you found to a detective in the Sheriff's office, and it was enough to push the DA to get a warrant. Now we just have to hope they can find what you found and more. So how did Justin respond?"

"He was livid! He tried to argue and block them, but you can't stop three big guys with a search warrant to back them up. Here's the best part, they concurrently had agents sent to his home and his vehicle, so they are leaving nothing to chance."

"That makes me think they had more than what I gave them. The detective I've been working with said they were looking for other suspects. Maybe they were on to Justin as well."

Arthur looked confused and said, "What do you mean the detective you've been working with? You never mentioned that. I remember you said someone came to your office, but nothing more."

"I know, and that's because it's not normal procedure for a defense lawyer, but this guy came again and said even though there was a lot of evidence against you and the DA just wanted to wrap it up and convict you, they weren't convinced you were guilty. That's when he told me they were continuing to investigate the case *unofficially*."

Arthur paused in thought, then Layton asked, "What is it Arthur, you seem perplexed."

"Oh, I don't know. I just don't understand why the Sheriff's office would go to so much trouble. I mean if the case seems open and shut, they could just be done with it. Why would they give any extra effort to my case, like they are doing it for me? What am I to them, nothing really, right?"

"I see your point. I think it's because they want to get the right guy, the guilty party. Detective Burch seems like a straight up guy looking for the truth. He doesn't settle. The one thing that bothered him was that you don't seem to have motive for the crime."

"You could be right, but it does seem odd to me."

"Hey, Arthur, let's not make too much of it. Just focus on the possible outcome. This could mean your exoneration."

"Yes," he replied as he slapped his knee. "That's the goal. I will no longer question the motives. Take whatever I can get that clears my name."

Layton and Arthur spent the next several days anticipating the outcome of the search of Justin's records. They feared Justin became suspicious and worked to hide the evidence Arthur had uncovered, but Layton believed they could then pull out the receipts Arthur had kept at home for the investors' funds he did deposit should it come to that.

Arthur continued to go into the office as usual and did his best to act normal. He even told Justin he knew he was innocent and suggested someone may be trying to cast suspicion on both of them. Justin was agitated and irritable most of the time, and that solidified Arthur's belief that Justin was guilty of the crime Arthur was being accused of.

As Layton became antsy, she thought about contacting Detective Burch but decided against it. He had been forthright with her in the past, and she believed he would share information with her if he could. They just needed to be patient.

In the meantime, she continued to prepare her case for Arthur. Her opening statement was just about complete, and it focused on Arthur's clean record, lack of motive, and character witnesses. She still struggled with instilling doubt when it came to the evidence against him. That was going to prove to be difficult. The account records in Arthur's name provided a trail of financial transactions that the prosecution would use as primary evidence to prove Arthur took the money from investors and embezzled it.

Even if she has to present his case without any evidence to the contrary, she wondered if a jury would consider the evidence they have conclusive. To be conclusive, the evidence must be so strong and convincing that it is without contradiction or beyond any doubt. Should she have to present her case in court with what she has now, she would need to convince the jury there is doubt that Arthur committed the crime. The information Arthur and Ronnie provided about Justin is definitely a contradiction to the evidence against Arthur, but she can't use it, it has to be found by the district attorney.

As part of the discovery process, the prosecution is required to inform the defense about any new evidence they have that would have a bearing on the case. They would not be allowed to withhold the evidence and reveal it for the first time during the trial. The defense must have a chance to review the evidence prior to the start of the trial.

In the hopes she would soon get a call from the district attorney's office informing her of evidence found after the search of Justin's office, she prepared a motion to dismiss the charges against Arthur. She didn't want to leave anything to chance. She had a plan A, and a plan B. Plan A was to present Arthur's case with an emphasis on reasonable doubt given Arthur's clean record, character witnesses, and no credible motive. Plan B, the one she anticipated, was to motion to dismiss all charges.

Layton and Arthur sat side-by-side in the court-room at the table designated for the defense. She had received word that the district attorney's office had received new evidence impacting Arthur's upcoming trial and had received a package by currier the next day with copies for her to review. It was just what she expected. Justin would now be the prime suspect.

A court date had been set for another pretrial hearing where motions would be heard. They waited with hopeful anticipation.

After the Judge entered and all the formalities were presented, the Judge began, "At this time I would like to hear, first from the district attorney and then from the attorney for the defense."

The district attorney stood, "Your Honor. New evidence has come to our attention in the case against Arthur Bowles, evidence that strongly contradicts the evidence we have used to build our case against him, specifically related to the charges of embezzlement. We provided the evidence to Ms. Virnetti and the court."

The Judge looked at Layton, "Do you have anything to say, Ms. Virnetti?"

"Yes, Your Honor. After reviewing this new evidence, it is my belief that the evidence used to bring charges against my client no longer provides certainty of the facts. It suggests that my client did not commit the crime and may have been framed. In fact, it contradicts the evidence used to arrest my client. In light of this, I have prepared a motion to dismiss all charges against Arthur Bowles."

Layton approached the bench and handed the Judge the documents containing her motion to dismiss. She then returned to her seat next to Arthur.

After scanning the document for several minutes, the Judge began, "I tend to agree. I have reviewed all the evidence during the initial pretrial discovery as well as this evidence. Without a strong case against Mr. Bowles, it seems keeping a trial on the docket is unwarranted at this time. Does the district attorney's office believe in light of this new evidence that there is still sufficient evidence against Mr. Bowles to proceed with trial should I grant a continuance? Have you a motion to file for continuance?"

"No, your Honor, we do not. We have prepared a motion to dismiss the charges against Mr. Bowles and provide the document to you at this time."

After reviewing the document from the prosecution, the Judge dropped the gavel and declared Arthur's case dismissed due to lack of credible evidence.

Chapter Twenty Three

With the pre-trial complete, resulting in the charges against Arthur dismissed, Layton proposed they meet for dinner that evening to celebrate. She wanted to work in the office for a few hours to catch up on some loose ends with other cases and also felt she needed a little quiet time to herself to come down from the excitement of the last few days.

She chose a small restaurant outside of town. She hoped there wouldn't be any reporters there. She and Arthur needed to be left alone now, and she believed the focus of the press would shift to Justin and the new charges against him brought just this afternoon. She was right, but just to be safe, they would avoid the center of town.

Dinner was fabulous. For the first time in months, they were able to talk and enjoy each other's company as they had over the years. They both avoided talk around legal matters. Arthur admitted he had lost a few pounds stressing over his upcoming trial, and at this time, his stomach was welcoming a big meal.

Layton was surprised by what he ordered and how much he ate. It felt good to see him so relaxed and, after taking her last bite, she sat back and sank into her own calm knowing she succeeded in helping to exonerate her good friend, Arthur Bowles.

They ordered an after dinner drink of straight Kentucky bourbon on the rocks once the meal was complete and they continued to celebrate the Judge's decision in the case. It was fitting after all they had been through over the past several months. To top it off, Arthur ordered cheesecake, dessert to share, much to Layton's objection.

Arthur continued their conversation, "Layton, there's something I want to say to you now that this awful ordeal is over. Thank you." He raised his glass, and she did as well. Then he continued, "In all sincerity, I mean it, but not just for your services as my attorney, for everything."

"What do you mean everything? What else is there to thank me for?"

Arthur looked down at his glass, he smoothed out the table cloth, wiped away a few crumbs that lay on top. Deep in thought, he was searching for words.

"Remember when I first moved here so many years ago?"

"Yes, of course, I remember."

"I didn't have a friend in the world. You became my friend, and I'll always be grateful for that."

"Oh, Arthur you don't have to thank me for that. It goes both ways, and I've valued your friendship too. Now having helped prove your innocence in this case, well that has been rewarding for me. And I can't ever repay you for your generosity in paying for a good portion of my college education."

"That's nothing, only money. What I'm talking about is what I've been able to experience knowing you for so many years. It goes beyond our friendship. Let me try to explain, but maybe I could have another drink."

He raised his hand to motion for their server and Layton agreed to have one more as they continued their conversation. They had spent so many days and evenings intensely working on his case that this evening was meant to be lingered over.

"I want you to know how much I enjoyed watching you grow up and being involved in your life. I would have loved to have a family, but that just wasn't my fate in life. Sharing your teen years as we walked to school together and fishing on Saturday, well that meant so much to me. The discussions we had were so rich and full, and I loved seeing you form your views and hear about your dreams for your life. I was so happy when you decided to come home and set up your practice here. You've been such a joy in my life."

Puzzled, she asked, "Arthur is something wrong? You seem so intent on this. Why now?"

He laughed and tried to lighten the mood, "No, nothing's wrong. Maybe it's the booze. I just felt there were some things I wanted you to know. I guess this being falsely accused of a serious crime caused me to do a lot of thinking."

He paused in thought, then leaned in closer and continued, "Just one more thing I want to say and then we will finish our last drink with less serious conversation."

They clinked glasses, took a sip and then looking at her with his penetrating blue eyes he said, "You are like a daughter to me Layton, and I love you."

"Oh Arthur," she said through her tears, "I love you too." Then she wiped her eyes with her napkin and said, "Now, enough of this mushy stuff. Let's finish our drink and celebrate. So, what are your plans?"

"I don't know. I can't see myself selling real estate especially in this town."

"Why not? All the money was recovered, and Justin forced to pay restitution to the investors. He's going to jail for a few years, then will be on probation for several more years. We still need a real estate office and maybe the development could still be realized."

"You could be right, but people will never be able to trust me again even if the charges were dropped against me and Justin is in jail. Besides, I am wrung out from all this. I need to do something different, I need a change."

"I understand. Hey, I have an idea. How about private investigation with a little forensic accounting in the mix? You did a great job finding what we needed for your case. Among the three of us, you, Ronnie, and me, we could form a nice defense team always working for justice." They both laughed and downed the last bit of their drinks.

Things shifted back to normal for Layton as she began to focus more on other cases and Arthur spent some time cleaning out his desk at the real estate office that remained closed for the time being. He had no plans of ever returning to selling real estate. What he would do now, he didn't know. He only knew what he didn't want. He didn't want to work in real estate, and he didn't want to live in this town.

He and Layton spoke on the phone and occasionally met for coffee. With their client attorney relationship ended, they were free to go back to being friends. Layton had missed that while working on his case and preparing for the trial. She was so focused on getting him off, felt she had to put their friendship aside for a while.

After several weeks of hard work catching up on other cases and getting back to securing new clients, she decided it was time to take a break and leave work early. *Time to visit and old friend and see if he will join me for dinner,* she thought as she left the office one Friday afternoon.

She headed towards Arthur's house. She decided not to call because she wanted to surprise him. As she approached the house, she saw the *For Sale* sign in the front yard. With no local real estate office currently open, the sign was that of a national brand. She was disappointed, but not surprised after what he said at their dinner celebration. She knew he needed a change, that he didn't want to stay here and definitely didn't want to work in that real estate office.

She hoped he would have dinner so they could talk and she could learn about his plans. When she approached the front porch, she noticed no lights were on and after ringing the bell with no answer, she moved to the picture window to take a peek inside. Immediately she noticed how bare the front room was. No furniture, no curtains, just a few stacked boxes that must have been packed. She could see they were sealed with tape. It appeared Arthur was gone. She quickly took out her cell phone and called his number. After two rings a voice began, "You have reached an out-of-service number. Please check the nu...." She stopped the call and tried again, same thing.

She sat down on the front steps in shock and wondered what had happened. Why would he leave like that without saying good-bye? She thought back to the last time she saw him. They met for a brief lunch during the work week, and he never mentioned anything about leaving. She wondered if he had known then what he was planning to do and why, if that was the case, he didn't' tell her. She knew he wanted a change, but this was drastic, and after all he said she meant to him.

She thought, *Why, why now, like this? I don't understand, and I need to know. I need to know where he is, how to contact him. I can't believe I'll never see him again or talk to him. Hopefully, he'll contact me after he gets where he's going. That's right, he will contact me, I'm sure of it....*

Part Three

Ellie

Chapter Twenty Four

Eleanor Gable was having a good day. At the age of seventy eight, she considered herself pretty fit, still able to take her two-mile walk around her Tennessee property without becoming too fatigued. She loved early morning. She felt the crisp air on her cheeks. The birds were lively in the trees as they voiced their impression of the new day with song.

Her property totaled thirty acres of land with her home right in the center providing a great deal of privacy. Privacy she enjoyed over her adult life, but also necessary for one critical reason.

Along her walking route, she passed by several small buildings used for a variety of purposes. The garden shed with all the essential tools to cultivate the grounds which included flower beds, shrubs, and hedges. There was a small garage next to the house that stored a small tractor with various attachments for mowing, digging, and tilling. There was a play house that provided hours of enjoyment in years past for her granddaughter, Ellie.

The main house had an attached, two-car garage for her vehicles, but in the back, south east corner of the property was another, smaller garage, run down, boarded up, in all appearances as if unused, abandoned. Eleanor rarely gave it a thought as she strolled by, but today was different, she was feeling reflective. She stopped at the building, gave a sigh, and then decided to go inside. At the back of the twenty foot by twenty foot structure, there was an access door not much taller than her five foot, three inch frame. It was slightly hidden by overgrown brush and weeds, but she pushed them away, unlocked the door and went inside.

She slowly pulled back an old tarp and revealed a treasure. As she ran her hand across the side of a vehicle, the glossy, flawless finish under her fingers began an emotion that traveled all the way through to her heart. What she felt was an intense pride knowing she had received this treasure and placed it here, hidden, for her granddaughter, Ellie, to one day find.

When Eleanor returned to the house, she prepared some breakfast and decided to call her lawyer as she finished her second cup of coffee.

"Hello, Eleanor, how are you? Well, I hope." Her lawyer, Ralston Hayes, inquired as he greeted her call.

"I'm doing fine, Ralston. Fit as a fiddle. I was just calling to check in. Is everything in order per my instructions at our last meeting regarding my final wishes?" She asked with a commanding tone in expectation that his answer would confirm what she already knew.

"Yes, yes indeed, Eleanor, everything is set, but I suspect you'll be around for a good long while." He replied.

"Right you are!" she answered. "I do, however, want to be prepared when my time comes. As you know, I MUST ensure my Miss Ellie is taken care of and..." she paused briefly, "receives what is rightfully hers."

"I understand, and you are smart to do this now. Then you can relax for the rest of your years."

"And the letter?" she asked.

"Yes, I have the letter. It is sealed and in the office safe. As you instructed, I have not read it, and I never will, but will keep it ready to distribute if necessary."

"Very good," she replied.

They ended their conversation with brief good-byes. Eleanor sat back, put her feet up, and took her last few sips of coffee fully satisfied that she had things in proper order.

Chapter Twenty Five

Ellie Gable, Attorney at Law, the words etched on the glass on the top half of the door in a modest office building in downtown Atlanta. She specialized in cases involving women who found themselves in a difficult situation, abused by their wealthy husbands, fearing the money and power their husbands possessed would prevent them from getting out of the marriage. Ellie knew differently and helped them secure their financial futures while protecting them from more abuse. She did not, however, encourage them to be greedy. She wanted clients that were good, honest people. She used the threat of a high dollar settlement as leverage and negotiated something more reasonable so that her clients could live comfortably and move on to start a new, safe and secure life for themselves.

Most of her clients were women who stayed home to manage the household and raise the children while their husbands pursued high-power careers. They were expected to give cocktail and dinner parties, attend charity events, and accompany their husbands on business trips when it was deemed necessary in support of their advancement. In short, her clients' lives were not their own. They were dependent on their husbands, and some endured years of verbal, emotional or physical abuse prior to seeking a divorce.

Yet some were not abused at all. They were basically unhappy, unfulfilled and wanted a different life feeling lost after their children grew up and began their own lives. They realized they had forgotten and forgone their own dreams and desires as they helped others around them realize theirs.

Linda Jenkins, a recent client, was a perfect example. She came to Ellie's office over a year ago asking for representation in her divorce case. She was married with two grown daughters and a husband who refused to allow her to pursue a career. She explained how she had tried to make the marriage work, but her husband had made it clear he wanted no changes now that she had an opportunity to do something for herself. He believed her role in life was to continue as a housewife, left to take care of him, their home, and support his career, rather than choose one for herself.

Linda described her devastation at the realization her husband wouldn't budge, leaving her no choice but to file for divorce and make a life on her own. Like most of the women Ellie represented, Linda came to her with no financial ability to pay. Her husband had complete control of all funds. In some cases, attorneys refuse to take the case without an initial retainer. Linda had consulted with two attorneys before meeting with Ellie, and she was surprised and pleased to learn Ellie was different. She worked without payment until the case was complete and the divorce was final. Her fees were part of the divorce agreement in the financial settlement between her client and the husband.

Unfortunately, this meant Ellie didn't always get paid. In some cases, her client would withdraw and stay in the marriage, or the husband would work out a settlement through his lawyer that his wife would need to agree to without independent representation. The later, typically ended with an agreement that favored the husband.

Having just finished wrapping up Linda's case, Ellie decided to treat herself to her favorite take out meal, a bottle of wine, and a relaxing evening at home to celebrate this latest victory. A job well done, she thought, but more importantly, a life changing outcome for her client.

After dinner, she settled into an overstuffed sofa with a magazine, jazz music on Pandora, and a refill of her glass of wine. Her solitude was interrupted when her cell phone rang.

"Hi, Grandma El. How are you?" she said when she saw the incoming call was from Eleanor.

"Well, Miss Ellie, I'm doing pretty well today. I had a nice walk around the property and then wrapped up some business with Ralston, my attorney. What are you up to tonight?"

"I'm relaxing with a magazine and a bottle of wine. Just finished up a difficult case with good results and feeling the need to chill a bit."

"Good for you! That's my girl. What was the case?"

"Much of the same, a woman leaves her husband after the kids leave the nest and are settled except this one didn't involve any abuse, and the husband was taken by surprise. He was successful with a full life. She wanted to pursue something, education, a career, anything as long as it was just for her and he wouldn't allow it. He said she needed to continue her volunteer work and take care of him, the house, entertain his business associates, on and on. He was shocked that she wanted to go through with the divorce and make a life for herself."

"Phew, that doesn't sound right. Hard for me to understand since I was a working mother and had a rewarding teaching career."

"Yes, I know. These women live such different lives, but all that money doesn't make them any happier than the rest of us."

"That's for sure, Ellie, it doesn't, and now look at her, she's divorced. Does she have any plans?"

"Nothing solid, but she knows she wants to do something with her life. I'm thinking of offering her a job."

"Really? Doing what? I hope you aren't just feeling sorry for her."

At that, Ellie laughed and said, "Don't worry, Grandma El, I have a plan. I've been getting pretty busy in my practice and was considering hiring an administrative assistant."

With skepticism, Eleanor asked, "Does she have the right skills or education to do the job?"

"Not on paper, but I think she can do the job. Before getting married, and I know this was several years ago, she went to a business college and earned a two-year degree in office procedures. But the important thing is the work she's done over the years. She's a super organizer heading up committees for several charity events, and she's served on a few boards, run meetings, things like that. Her organizational skills are stellar."

"That sounds promising."

"The way she presented information and documents to me when I was preparing to represent her in her divorce case, well that was enough for me to see she's got skills I can use. I even see her becoming a paralegal someday with the right training and experience."

"Sounds like you've given this a lot of thought. What's her name?"

"Her name is Linda, and she was married pretty young, so she's in her mid-forties."

"Do you think she would take the job?"

"I honestly don't know, but I think I could convince her to give it a try. I tell ya Grandma El, we really clicked working on her case. She was a big help to me."

"Sounds like it's worth a shot. I better let you go now and get back to your relaxing evening. Let me know what you decide and how things go."

"I will. Thanks for calling. Maybe I can bring Linda on board and free up some time while she covers the phones to visit soon."

"Oh, Ellie, I would love that. Hopefully soon!"

The following Monday, Ellie called her former client, Linda and asked if she could stop by her office sometime. Linda had purchased a townhouse in a nice suburb just outside of Atlanta, and she was trying to make the best of her new freedom but was feeling a little lost at times. She hadn't yet figured out what she wanted to do with the rest of her life. Her children were now on their own with full lives. She knew there would be opportunities for her to spend time with them and, if they chose to start families, she could help with grandkids, but for now, she needed to do something for herself and her new life.

When her attorney called, she thought there must be some loose ends to tie up, maybe documents to sign. She was looking forward to seeing Ellie again. They had spent much time together working on her case, something she had missed once it was complete.

She was relieved when the divorce was final, and everything was settled, but working through the process had given her purpose and started to build some of the self-esteem she had lost over the years watching her husband succeed in his career. To Linda, Ellie seemed genuine when she told Linda she believed the assistance she provided on the case was a big part of the successful outcome.

She entered the Law office in good spirits, happy to see Ellie and happy to have a reason to fix her hair and makeup and dress up a little, having somewhere to be today. After the meeting she planned on doing a little shopping in the City.

"Linda, so good to see you again. Sit down. Can I get you some coffee?"

"Sure, I would love some. Is there something we still need to wrap up on my case?"

"No, nothing like that, the case is completely closed. I have something else I want to talk to you about, and I'm hoping you'll at least hear me out before giving me an answer."

"I'm all ears."

"Well, I have a job opportunity for you, working here with me. I've been toying with the idea of hiring an administrative assistant leading into some paralegal work, and I think you would be perfect."

Linda was surprised and let out a laugh, "That's funny. Me? I don't think so. I don't have that kind of experience."

"I'm serious about this. I saw how you pulled together information I needed for your case and with quick turnaround after I requested it. Then there's all the work you've done with your charities, the kids' school organizations. I could go on and on, but I think you can see my point. Like I said, consider it. Open your mind to it and let me know what you think."

"All I can say is thank you for thinking of me, Ellie. I'm a little stunned right now. It's not at all what I expected, but I'm thrilled you would take a chance on me and give me this opportunity. I hadn't made any plans yet so I can consider it. Can you give me a little time to give it some thought?"

"Yes, of course, Linda. I can see this comes as a surprise and I know you have a new life ahead of you. You have options, and I'm sure you want to make sure you choose wisely. Even if you want to do this on a trial basis, I would be open to that. Say six months or so, and if it isn't working for you or you find something else you want to pursue, I would understand with no hard feelings. Take the time you need and let me know what you decide."

"I sure will. It won't be long though, I don't want to leave you hanging. I do so appreciate the offer, and I'll be in touch."

In anticipation of Linda accepting her offer, Ellie began to set up a reception area in her outer office. She ordered a desk, chair, computer, and miscellaneous office supplies. She'd decided that even if Linda didn't come to work for her, she would need to hire someone to help her manage the growing client list and she needed someone soon.

She hoped Linda would take her up on her offer and had little doubt it was the right thing to do. She admitted she wanted to help Linda out and give her some purpose, but her gut was telling her she would benefit from this offer of employment to Linda too.

After a week went by, she heard from Linda who accepted the offer with much excitement. They agreed she would start the following Monday. Ellie was pleased to watch Linda as she organized her desk in the reception area of the office and she knew this was going to be the beginning of a wonderful working relationship. With Linda in place, Ellie could now look forward to a visit to Grandma El at her house in Tennessee.

Ellie approached the long driveway leading to her grandmother's house with delight. She hadn't seen Eleanor in over a year, and she missed her. They talked on the phone often, and some of their conversations lingered on, but nothing could replace a visit to her childhood home spending time with her beloved Grandma El.

She had been looking forward to this visit for the past few months as she worked to position herself in her law practice to allow her to take a break. She had hired Linda, her administrative assistant, and began training her so that she could cover the office for just a week or two. Ellie felt confident the office was in good hands.

As she pulled into the driveway circle in front of the house, her grandmother came out on to the front porch with outstretched arms, all smiles.

They embraced, then walked arm in arm into the house for a cup of tea and a long conversation. Eleanor suggested Ellie's bags could wait.

"I'm so glad you came, Ellie."

"Me too. I've missed you so much and not being here last Christmas was so weird."

Eleanor rolled her eyes and responded, "I know what you mean. I had to go and take my friend up on the offer to go on that holiday cruise. I wouldn't have done it, but she had just lost her husband, and it pulled at my heartstrings."

"I understood, but I hated spending the holidays in Atlanta. There were a few of friends I got together with, but it's just not the same as celebrating with family and out here away from the city."

"Well, this year we will be together for the holidays. No more holiday cruises, you have my word! And I was thinking I might come up to Atlanta and spend a few days with you in a few months. You can keep working, and I'll occupy myself in the day, but we can have dinner and spend some evenings together."

"That sounds terrific," Ellie responded.

They spent the next couple of hours talking and planning. Ellie filled Eleanor in on how things were going at the office with Linda and Eleanor gave a summary of what she had been doing with her various activities with clubs, hobbies, and friends. They had a late dinner then Ellie unpacked and went to bed early promising to rise at six to join her grandmother for her weekly trip to the farmer's market to get supplies for the week.

Chapter Twenty Six

"Grandma El," Ellie said as they relaxed on the front porch with a couple of tall glasses of iced tea, "what are your plans for the coming years? Do you ever think about selling the place and downsizing to a townhome or apartment?"

"Sometimes, but I can't because..." she stopped after realizing she couldn't truthfully finish her sentence.

"What do you mean you can't?" Ellie asked surprised.

"I didn't mean I can't, I meant I couldn't, couldn't leave this place as long as I'm healthy and able to keep up with it." She stopped and hoped her answer satisfied her granddaughter.

"I understand, but I was hoping someday you might want to move to Atlanta and be near me. What about that?"

"Sounds wonderful being close to you, but I'm happy here, and my life is here. I have my friends, activities, and most of all, my memories." She looked to the side thinking.

"Yes, I see, but that look you just gave almost seemed sad not joyful."

"Not sadness, but a mixture of happy memories and sad memories. Everyone's life is a mixed bag. We all have that. I remember the years fondly with your grandfather, raising your father and then welcoming my daughter-in-law and you into the family. Then when they had their accident, it was deep sadness for you and for me. Then, what followed were wonderful years that we had together. So you see, my memories, no matter what, are all here, and I want to stay here with those memories." Ellie nodded and tapped Eleanor's hand. She couldn't speak as the words her grandmother spoke caused her to fight back the tears.

"Now," Eleanor replied. "Let's go up to the attic and sort through a few boxes that I want you to check out and see if you want to bring anything back to remind you of home."

Ellie started with a box of photographs. "Hey, here's Mom and Dad's wedding pictures. Can I have one of these?" Eleanor took one of the photos and lightly touched it with her fingertips. She didn't say anything for a long time. "You okay Grandma El?"

"Yes, I'm fine, just thinking how much I wish you knew your parents. You missed so much." Ellie put her arm around Eleanor's shoulder and said, "I know I missed the things I would have done with my parents, but I can't *miss* them per se because you can't miss what you never knew."

"You know, you're right. You were so young and have no memory of them. Miss Ellie, you sure do have a way of seeing things in a positive light." They hugged. "That's my girl. Now you take any photos you wish. I won't be here forever, and they will all go to you someday anyway."

"Ha!" Ellie exclaimed, "You, I am sure, will be around for a long time. You're too stubborn to leave this world for many years, and besides, I need you, you old coot." They both laughed as they remembered Eleanor loved to call men she considered getting on in age 'old coot' when they tried to flirt with her after her husband died, men she would have nothing to do with. She always said her heart belonged to one man.

"Well," Eleanor said, "I will leave you to your work searching through photographs and head downstairs to get started on dinner. I'm making one of your favorites, beef stew with buttermilk biscuits and for dessert, cherry pie."

"Ooo, yes! I can't wait," Ellie exclaimed.

After Eleanor left, Ellie continued to look through the photographs. There were several of her parents before she was born and then a larger number of her in the first few years of her life, many with her parents. She guessed Eleanor must have been keen on taking photos at every family gathering.

Next came the ones with just her again, no parents. Her first day of preschool, the first day of kindergarten, swimming lessons, music lessons, school plays, all the way to high school graduation, prom night, and college. Her entire life so far was captured in this one box of photos.

She was happy her grandma El hadn't progressed to the digital age where photos where kept on the camera, Facebook, computer, or a disc. Her grandmother said that photos should be held in your hand, passed around, and reminisced over. Ellie remembered the year she gave Eleanor a digital camera for Christmas. She taught her grandmother how to use it and save photos on her computer. Eleanor loved the camera and the ease of use. No longer did she need to buy film, but she refused to only save the pictures on her computer. She always had them printed. Said she wanted to see them that way just like she wanted to continue to read books in print form, no eBook for her.

Ellie paused at one photo, the one of her and Eleanor on her high school graduation day. They posed in front of the auditorium stage, she in cap and gown holding her diploma, Eleanor all dressed up with a big smile on her face, beaming with pride. Ellie thought, *Oh Grandma El, what a wonderful childhood you gave me. Out of tragedy you rose up and did all in your power to raise a child and make her life the best it could be. My parents must have watched from above with some comfort knowing they had left their only child in good hands. Yet, sometimes I feel as if they aren't really gone. I guess that's because you kept them alive for me all these years. You never let me forget William and Suzanne. You made sure I got to know them through these photographs and sharing your memories. Oh, how I loved the stories you told about them. My father, as he was growing up, then his life with Suzanne and their baby girl.*

Running her fingers over a photograph of her parents, side-by-side, Suzanne holding their baby girl, she thought. *I wish I could remember you both. I wish we had had more time together, but I'm glad Grandma El kept you alive in my heart, as you both were in hers.*

She finished choosing a few photos to take home but didn't want to disturb the box very much. She wanted just a few to put in a collage-type frame to hang on her wall. She felt the majority of them should stay here with Grandma El.

"How'd you make out?" Eleanor asked as Ellie entered the kitchen. "Did you take a nice batch of photos to take home?"

"Not too many, just a few to put in a frame and hang on the wall."

"Okay, but remember if you ever want more, you know where to find them."

Saturday morning, Ellie awoke early and decided since it was the last day of her visit, she would get up and take a walk around the property, alone. She strolled easily and savored each breath of fresh air, each sound, each vision filled with memories of her childhood here with Grandma El. Time briefly stood still. She wondered if she would ever come back here on a permanent basis. It had never been her intent, but these past several days had provided a renewed connection, and she felt strangely changed by it.

Looking through the attic and the family photos caused her to think a lot about her childhood and her grandmother. When you're living it, you just take everything day-by-day.

As she made her way around, she thought about how big this property was and how her grandmother was getting up there in age. She wondered how Eleanor could continue to take care of this place. Would she have the energy, and could she afford it financially? She had to ask herself, why was grandma El so adamant about keeping this place? Ellie didn't want to pry, but there may come a time when she would need to step in and make sure Eleanor was taken care of as she got older.

Most young people have parents just twenty or thirty years older than they, but she had Eleanor that was over forty years her senior. It made her situation different. As a lawyer, she was aware of the various matters that needed to be addressed as people aged. She then reminded herself, Grandma El has her own attorney, and as independent and capable as she is, she must have everything taken care of with Mr. Hayes.

As her walk around the property came to an end, she started to shift her thoughts to her work and her life in Atlanta. She was looking forward to getting back to her practice and her work with her new assistant, Linda.

With her bags stowed in the trunk of her car, Ellie was ready to head back to her life in Atlanta. Grandma El gave her a lingering hug, then returned to the porch and waved as her granddaughter drove away. She entered the house thinking, *I'm feeling suddenly drained. I must have overdone it with Ellie's visit, and I'll take it easy this afternoon.*

Chapter Twenty Seven

When Ellie returned to the office Monday morning, Linda was already there at her desk drinking her second cup of coffee, ready for another day to begin.

"Wow, Linda, you're here bright and early. How did things go while I was gone?"

"Things went pretty well. I did some organizing around the office, ordered supplies and coffee, made some appointments for you with new clients, two of whom were walk-ins."

"You've been busy."

"Yeah and I had to talk with the new ones for a bit, you know not just make appointments. They were pretty distraught, and I couldn't just rush them out."

"How did that go?"

"Well, at first I hesitated because, um, I'm not a lawyer. I'm not you. They both just started unloading, and I could definitely relate with my experience with divorce."

"Right about that," Ellie agreed.

"So as the conversation continued, I became more comfortable."

"I'm sure you did well, possibly even better than I when I had my first few clients in these situations."

"First I just listened and then I tried to reassure them that you could help them with the legal matters. I also let them know that I was divorced and that I'd been right where they are at this moment, that better days were coming." Ellie poured a cup of coffee and sat in the chair next to Linda's desk.

"I'm so glad I hired you, Linda. You're just what this practice needed. I hope you're happy you came to work here."

"Yes, I certainly am. Now let's go over the appointments you have scheduled. The first one is this morning at 11 and....."

As the day came to a close, Ellie asked Linda to come into her office for a little talk before leaving for the day.

"Linda, I wanted to run something by you before you leave."

"Okay, shoot."

"First off, you've been doing great here, and I want you to know how pleased I am with your work. You've been such a big help to me, my practice is growing, and that wouldn't be possible without you here."

"Thanks for that. I wasn't sure how things would work out when I took this job. I mean, it had been so long since I was in the workforce and I'll tell you the truth, I was scared."

"Really?" Ellie said with surprise, "You didn't show it. You seemed confident right from the start."

"Apparently, I'm good at acting too," she replied with a wink.

"Apparently," Ellie replied with a chuckle. "Now, what I want to know is, do you want to do more?"

"More? Like what?" Linda asked.

"Do you have any interest in becoming a paralegal?"

"I would love to if you think I can do it."

"Of course I do. You would have to get into a program, and there are several options…" At which point Linda jumped up from her chair and headed for her desk in the outer office.

"Hold on," she said, "I know, and I did some research on that very subject while you were gone."

She returned with a folder and proceeded to go through several training programs she had found having attached each one with a cover sheet outlining the type of program, length of time to complete, and cost.

"Wow, you have done your homework on this. This is awesome."

"Thanks. I know you mentioned the possibility of this when you first hired me. I had no idea how long it would take to accomplish, and I was curious, so I did some checking. I think I like this one that combines classroom attendance with online courses. It's offered at the local university, and I think some face-to-face instruction is beneficial, but the online portion could be something I could work on at the office when my work is caught up."

"I like that too. This is your thing, so I want you to choose what works best for you, and of course, you can do as much course work as possible right here from the office. And I'll pay for everything, tuition, books, supplies, everything."

"Oh, wow, that's very generous, but I don't expect you to do that. It seems like too much. Maybe I should pay for at least part of it."

Ellie paused in thought, tapping her pen on the desk a few times then responded with something lawyer like, "I'll make a deal with you. I'll pay full freight, and you sign a document stating if you leave here within two years of completing the program, you pay me back for all costs."

"Deal," Linda replied and reached out her hand to shake on it then continued, "We've been so busy catching up on work and talking shop, I haven't even asked you how your grandmother's doing."

"She's great. We had a wonderful visit."

"Glad to hear it, but now you look a little sad. Was it hard leaving after a good visit?"

Ellie didn't speak for a few moments as she thought about what Linda just said.

"Not sad, but mindful."

"What do you mean?" Linda asked.

"I was thinking about a lot of different things. It started when Grandma El wanted me to go to the attic and look through old photographs and take some back with me. We talked a lot about my parents."

"I know they died when you were young, but how did they die?"

"They were in a car accident."

Linda could sense Ellie didn't want to elaborate so she didn't ask anything further.

"Then," Ellie continued without any more details about the accident. "Before I left, I took a walk around the property and thought about my childhood there with my grandmother. I kept having some strange feelings."

"What kind of feelings?"

"Hard to explain, but there were times when I thought about my parents and felt they were still with us."

"Yeah, I know what you mean. After we lose someone close to us, we feel their spirit in our presence. It's common to feel that way. I was very close to a great Aunt of mine, and after she died, I could sometimes feel her with me. It's a good feeling though."

"I know, but that's not really what it was. It wasn't like they were with me in spirit. Anyway, then I was thinking about my grandmother and how she was like a parent, but older and wouldn't be alive for as much of my life as my parents would have been if they were alive. I've always been a logical thinker, less of a feeler, but this trip surprised me. I seemed to be feeling so many things." Ellie laughed, then said with a lighter tone, "I had to get back to work to shake off the sentimental aura that plagued me."

"That can be taken care of here with all the work we have ahead of us. Your practice is really growing."

"And that's just how we like it."

"Right," Linda stated as she got up and headed back to her office, "I think I'll head out now and let you get back to work."

Chapter Twenty Eight

"Good afternoon, Gable Attorney office," Linda stated as she answered the phone.

"Hello. Is this Linda?"

"Yes, it is. How may I help you?"

"Linda, this is Eleanor Gable, Ellie's grandmother. Is Ellie available?"

"No, I'm sorry Mrs. Gable. She's out of the office seeing clients. Can I have her call you when she comes back?"

"Yes, please if she's not too busy. Otherwise, tell her I can talk with her this evening."

"I'll give her the message, but I'm sure you will hear from her this afternoon. I've heard a lot about you Mrs. Gable and know how dear you are to Ellie."

"Please, Linda, call me Eleanor. I've heard a lot about you too, and let me say, I'm really pleased that Ellie hired you. You've been a big help to her in that office."

"I hope so, but I'm the one that benefited from this job. It came to me just at a time when I needed it desperately. Not financially, but I was at a turning point in my life, and this was the direction and support I needed to build confidence in myself."

"And my Miss Ellie was just the one to assist with that."

"I hope I get to meet you some day, Eleanor. I hear you are a remarkable woman."

They both laughed, and Eleanor replied, "Well, I don't know about that, but you may get your chance soon. I was hoping to take a trip to Atlanta in the near future. That's why I wanted to talk to my granddaughter."

"That's great news. She'll be excited I'm sure."

"It was nice talking to you, Linda. Hopefully we will see you soon."

It was a few weeks before Eleanor made the trip to Atlanta. Even though Eleanor suggested Ellie could work during her visit, Ellie didn't want to leave her on her own every day. She planned her schedule so that she could take a day or two off with a couple of afternoons free as well. Linda was happy to cover the office, and Ellie was nearby and on call should any emergency arise.

Eleanor planned a week and a half visit with a weekend in the middle, at Ellie's suggestion, so that they could spend Saturday with Linda too. Ellie wanted Grandma El to get to know Linda, and Linda was looking forward to spending time with Ellie's grandmother.

"Okay, Miss Ellie," Eleanor said as she flopped in the chair and put her feet up on the ottoman. "I need you to go back to work Monday so I can get a day of rest. Today was so much fun, but I am *exhausted*."

"I hear ya. It was a great day, but maybe I packed too many activities into one day, or I should say Linda did. She's the one that planned everything."

"It was a great day, and I know you wanted to take advantage of the time the three of us spent together, but I'm feeling my age after all that sightseeing and shopping. At least she planned a meal and afternoon snack to recharge a bit." They both laughed.

"So, what do you think of Linda?"

"She's super. Her organizational skills shined today, so I can see why you thought she'd be good as an administrative assistant, but on a personal level, she seems very genuine. I'm glad you offered her the job and that she accepted. I wasn't sure at first. You know I questioned whether you might just be feeling sorry for her."

"I know you did, I remember, and you made me think. You've always been good at that, you know, asking me questions that make me think rather than giving me your opinion or telling me what to do."

"I never liked telling an adult what to do. I'd rather respect their decision."

"Right, but you were that way even when I was growing up. I think it's because you were a teacher and you treated your students that way. You wanted them to learn even from their mistakes."

"You've figured me out, Miss Ellie. No fooling you girl. Now, what should we do about dinner? How about we order a pizza and have a couple of beers?"

"Sounds great!"

Monday morning Ellie entered the office just before nine. Linda was already at her desk with her second cup of coffee working on some coursework from her current paralegal class. She looked up when Ellie came in.

"What are you doing here? I thought today was a day off with Eleanor."

"She kicked me out, sent me to work today. Said we wore her out Saturday and wanted a day to relax. And it didn't help that I wanted to play a round of golf on Sunday."

"Oh boy. Did you do 18 holes?"

"No. We did nine on the executive course, but still, she was tired out."

"A day at home to herself will do her good. When does she go home, I forgot?"

"She's leaving Thursday. We have two more days together, then I'll see her again at Christmas. We're both looking forward to that."

"That sounds nice," Linda replied with no enthusiasm.

"I think we'll close the office because I'm usually not too busy at that time. People don't typically start divorce proceedings until after New Year's. Seems they try to get through the holidays, especially if there are children involved. What are your plans for the holidays this year?"

Linda said with a sigh, "I don't know. This is the first Christmas since the divorce was final. I wish I could just skip right over it all. I hear from my daughter that Stan already has a girlfriend, nothing too serious, but I'm sure she will be with him. The kids will probably spend Christmas at his house. I can't believe I have to say that. You know how he kept the house that used to be our home. I'm glad we're divorced, and I love my new home, but there are so many good memories at that house with the kids growing up."

"Maybe you should see the kids on a weekend before or after Christmas at your place and exchange gifts, then do something different on your own over Christmas." And then Ellie thought of the perfect holiday bonus and gift for Linda.

"That's a great suggestion. I'll give it some more thought, but first I have to get through Thanksgiving."

"Oh, that's right. Just so you know, if you find yourself alone, come with me to Grandma El's. I'm sure she would love to have us both."

"That's sweet of you, but that's family time for the two of you."

"I get it, but the invitation is always open. I mean it!"

Chapter Twenty Nine

"Good morning, Linda," Ellie said as she entered the office. "Did you have a nice thanksgiving?"

"Yes. It was wonderful. I hosted at my place. Just the girls and their boyfriends. We ate a huge meal and, then after cleaning up, had cocktails and played board games. It was one of the nicest Thanksgivings I've had in a long time."

"That's great!"

"How about you? How is Grandma El?"

"She's doing well. We decided on roast chicken for just the two of us. And guess what she's decided on for a new hobby? You'll never guess."

"I'm sure I can't, but I bet I won't be surprised."

"She's into making home brew!"

"You're kidding. How was it?"

"I thought it was pretty good. She had three batches, and my favorite was the IPA. You know she even grew her own hops over the summer?"

"Good Lord. That woman is super cool."

"Yeah, she is. We had a great time and made our plans for Christmas. Now, after I get settled and you have a few minutes, come into my office. I have some thoughts about our time off during December and New Year's."

Ellie and Linda worked at their desks for about an hour catching up on emails and phone calls. Linda peeked her head in Ellie's office and said, "Is this a good time to talk?"

"Perfect. Let's get a cup of coffee and sit at the table."

"I'll get the coffee," Linda replied. When she came back with two cups, she noticed a small package on the table. It looked like a tie box and was wrapped in Christmas paper with a red satin ribbon.

They both sat down, and Ellie started, "I was thinking we should close the office for about ten days beginning the day before Christmas Eve then come back after New Year's. Grandma El and I want to decorate the house together, so I want to get there early on Christmas Eve or even the night before."

"That sounds great, but I don't really need that much time off if you want me to keep the office open for a few days."

"Actually, you do need that much time. Here, open this," she said as she pushed the package across the table to Linda.

"What's this? It looks like a Christmas gift. Isn't it a bit early?"

"Yup," Ellie replied. "It sure is. You'll see why when you open it."

Linda carefully removed the ribbon and unwrapped the box. Inside was an envelope with a picture on the front of a beach, palm tree, and a beach chair. She opened the envelope. Inside was a ticket for a five day cruise. Linda read it out loud, "*five day Caribbean cruise, December 23rd through December 27th. Embarking from Miami Florida. All inclusive.* Are you kidding me?"

"No, but you have to know it's fully refundable or it can be rescheduled. I did it that way just in case your plans change between now and then, and you decide to spend Christmas with the family. I had to give it to you now because they need two weeks' notice to cancel this reservation and schedule your trip at a different time. So it's up to you."

Linda jumped up from her chair, moved around the table and gave Ellie a big hug.

"Thank you so much! It's perfect. I will use it as is. The kids are spending Christmas as planned at their father's, and I'm on my own. This will be just what I need to take my mind off it." She returned to her seat and picked up the ticket again.

Ellie smiled and said, "I'm so glad. Enjoy! So, you're getting together with the kids over New Years?"

"Yup, New Year's Eve and they're staying with me at the townhouse overnight, then New Year's Day we'll go to a movie and out to eat....but wait...how did you know that?"

"I called one of the girls and told her about my plan for your gift, and she filled me in on the family plans so that I could time it right."

"You are something else, Ellie, and I thank you so much for this. You're so thoughtful."

"I hope you don't mind taking a cruise by yourself."

"Are you kidding me? I'm thrilled. I'm going to bring a couple of books, schedule a massage at the spa, and sun myself on the deck. Oh, I think it'll be fun and relaxing. And, you know, I hear they seat you with other passengers for meals, so I'm sure I'll meet some people. I thought about doing this after the divorce, just haven't gotten around to it. It will be an adventure."

Chapter Thirty

December 23rd finally arrived. With Linda safely dropped off at the airport with ample time to get through security and make her flight, Ellie began her drive to Grandma El's for the holidays. The law office would remain closed, and she and Linda would both return to work on January 2nd.

Traffic was a little heavier than most days during the week, but she knew the 24th would be even worse. She was glad she decided to make the trip today, giving her and her grandmother plenty of time to decorate the house for Christmas.

She turned her car radio streaming service to the *Holly* station, and her excitement began to build as she made her way to her childhood home in Tennessee.

Ellie and Eleanor enjoyed the next several days celebrating Christmas together. After Ellie arrived on the 23rd, they picked out a small tree on the property to cut down and spent the next few hours decorating. They reminisced about Christmases past. Ellie loved going through all the decorations. The ornaments especially, as they each held a memory for her. Some she made as a child, some she received on Christmas morning, and others her Grandmother had saved from William and Suzanne's home.

On New Year's Eve, Eleanor hosted a party with neighbors and friends. To surprise her granddaughter, she invited some of Ellie's friends from high school who still lived in the area. It was a fun time and a great way to ring in the New Year. Eleanor and Ellie enjoyed spending this time together, decorating, opening gifts, long walks around the property, long talks, and celebrating the New Year.

On her first day back at work, Ellie arrived early at the office. She was refreshed from the long period away and was looking forward to getting back into a routine. She made a pot of coffee, checked her phone and email messages, and decided on a plan for the day to get caught up. Linda entered the office a few minutes before nine.

"Ellie," she said. "You beat me in. How was your trip?"

"It was great, but who cares about mine," she replied with a chuckle. "How was the cruise?"

"It was awesome!" Linda exclaimed as she headed for the coffee pot. After pouring a cup, she sat in the chair across from Ellie's desk and proceeded to fill her in on the cruise, ending with, "I can't thank you enough for that gift. It was just what I needed. You were right, getting away over Christmas worked great and spending New Year's with the kids was wonderful."

"Did you meet a lot of people on the cruise?"

"I sure did. I was happy there were other loners on the cruise. I spent some time outside of meals with people I met, around the pool, going into ports, drinks at the night clubs, stuff like that. I made some friends, and we've even promised to get together again, maybe on another cruise."

"That's good to hear. Sounds like a great time. Maybe I'll give a cruise a try."

The Law office became very busy over the next few months with an increasing client base including divorce cases and other services needed after the divorces are final. Because many of the divorcees received hefty financial settlements, they needed assistance protecting their financial assets going forward.

Ellie Gable, Attorney at Law, was gaining an excellent reputation in Atlanta. She was known for her negotiating skills and her ability to put women at ease as they travelled through one of the most challenging times of their adult lives. Her work was rewarding, and now that Linda was on board, poised to complete her paralegal program, Ellie was positioned to grow her practice to the next level.

Ellie was enjoying diving into the practice, working longer days and on weekends. She was also planning to move into a larger office space as soon as Linda becomes a paralegal. The next step, hire an administrative assistant to replace Linda who would be promoted to paralegal with a nice pay raise.

In early September, Ellie decided to go into the office on Saturday morning. She had dinner plans that evening with a friend from college, and she wanted to get some work done before her night out. She loved Saturday mornings at the office. It was quiet. Few phones calls and no walk-ins enabled her to focus without interruption and get a lot of work accomplished.

She was currently working on a difficult case that involved physical abuse. Her client was living in a women's shelter with her young daughter, and the husband had influence with law enforcement, making it hard to prove the abuse. Linda had been interviewing neighbors and friends to see if she could find anyone that had witnessed the abuse or that their client had confided in after any abusive event. They found two, but one had subsequently denied the initial account. Ellie could only assume the witness feared retaliation from the husband. She needed to keep digging and find something to use as leverage with the husband to pressure him to succumb to his wife's demand for a divorce.

She was about to pick up the phone to make a call when her phone rang.

"Ellie Gable," she said as she answered the phone.

"Hello, Ellie. This is Ralston Hayes, your grandmother's attorney in Tennessee."

"Yes Mr. Hayes, I remember you. How are you?"

"I'm fine Ellie, but I have some news about Eleanor."

"News? Is she alright?" Ellie replied with concern.

"No, I'm afraid she's not, and I'm so sorry to have to tell you this over the phone, but your grandmother suffered a stroke early this morning. She was lost to us immediately, but didn't suffer in any way."

Ellie put her hand to her mouth, closed her eyes, briefly fighting back the tears, but a few began to well in her eyes.

Ralston waited for her to adjust to the shock, then continued, "She was such a gift to us all, but it was her time. I'm so sorry, Ellie, I know how close the two of you were given that she raised you from childhood."

"Yes, Mr. Hayes, we were very close, and I loved her so much."

"I suppose she listed me as her first contact since you lived out-of-town. I received word from the local authorities today. The woman who comes in once a week to help with house cleaning found her on the floor. It must have happened first thing because there was fresh coffee in the pot."

"This is such a shock, she has been so healthy."

"I know Ellie. You're right she was a very active, healthy woman. We can only be thankful she had so many good years and her death was without any suffering."

"That's true. I'm glad of that. Thank you so much for calling to let me know, Mr. Hayes. I know how much she relied on you for advice over the years and to handle her affairs."

"You're welcome Ellie, and again, I'm so sorry. Now, Eleanor did leave things all arranged with me including her final wishes for burial, but we can discuss that at a later time."

"I'll come to Tennessee right away, and we can get together."

"Fine, just let me know when you are settled, and you can come into the office. I have a few things to go over with you including her will, but her situation was not complicated so it won't be too involved."

Later that week, Ellie arrived in Bethel Springs, Tennessee, and drove straight to her grandmother's house. As she approached the long drive leading to the house, she was overcome with a mix of emotions. Joy and happiness as she returned home, the place she was raised by her Grandma El, and sadness at the realization she would never see her again. She was glad they had recently spent so much time together after she hired Linda to help in the office.

Eleanor brought Ellie home to raise after her parents were tragically killed in a car accident as they were returning from a trip to the state capital. Ellie was just under four years old. She never learned many of the details around her parent's accident, but apparently, a driver fell asleep at the wheel, crossed into her parents' lane, and their car went off the road into a wooded area and hit a tree. Her mother died en route to the hospital, and her father, after being listed in critical condition, died several hours later. The other driver was never found nor charged. Grandma El was always reluctant to talk about it.

When Ellie became an adult and a law student, she thought about why her grandmother didn't pressure the police to investigate the accident further or work harder to find the person who ran the car off the road, leaving the scene. Ellie knew from doing some research that her father had been a key witness against his boss who was involved in illegal business activities, but the accident was reported as unrelated to his upcoming testimony. Grandma El was such a strong, independent woman. Ellie never understood why she wasn't striving to find the answers and getting justice for her son and daughter-in-laws' deaths.

Ellie remembers one afternoon when they were having a cup of tea together, she began questioning her grandmother. She was home for a few weeks on a semester break, and her studies at law school had prompted her curiosity. She thought about her grandmother's response to her questions, "I would have liked to see the person responsible punished, but the police really had so little to go on, and remember, I had a three year old to raise by myself since I had lost your grandfather shortly before you were born."

Ellie did understand. Her grandmother did an excellent job raising her, and she knew so much warmth and joy in this house. As she walked through the rooms now, she thought about how alone she was and yet... she felt Eleanor's presence. Placing both hands on her arms as she crossed them in front of her body, she slowly moved about, and then found herself saying aloud, "Are you here Grandma El? I know you are. I can feel your love filling the room." It was difficult for her to be there alone with her Grandma El now gone.

Later that day Ellie arrived at Ralston Hayes' office. After the initial small talk was finished, Ralston began to discuss Eleanor's will.

"Well, Ellie, as I'm sure you are aware, you are the only living relative of Eleanor. Beyond just a few small financial gifts to her favorite charities, your grandmother has instructed me, through her will, and as the executor of her estate, to inform you that everything she owned is now yours. This consists of her house and property as well as all the contents of the buildings on the property.

In addition, she had a small life insurance policy of which you are the beneficiary, a checking and savings account, and she did keep a safety deposit box at the bank. I have the key, and I am to give that to you now. I was never told what the box contained, but in any case, its' contents are yours."

At this point, Ralston paused giving Ellie a chance to ask questions, and she said, "I'm sure everything in total is not financially substantial. My grandmother lived quite simply, but valued the property. I will honor her by showing great respect for her things."

Ralston then continued, "Yes, Ellie, I'm sure you will. Now, there is just one more thing I must discuss with you, a set of important instructions Eleanor gave me. I'll go over them with you now. Please don't misunderstand, your grandmother did not believe you would be in a hurry to sell everything off and take the money, but she seemed adamant that you consider things before selling. She, therefore, gave me the following conditions to your inheritance:

First, you must personally view the contents of the safe deposit box. Second, you cannot sell the house and land for a minimum of one year. And finally, you are to visit and see all of the property, including the outbuildings no matter what their condition.

Now, she does not stipulate that you live there or even keep the property after one year, but it was her wish that you spend some time there, see all there is to see, remember your life there with her, give yourself time and then decide what you want to do. Do you have any questions for me?"

"No," she answered slowly. "I'm just a little taken aback. I would never dream of selling everything quickly, and I have to wonder why she felt so strongly about the conditions."

"I don't know, but she was determined and sure about what she wanted. Please let me know if there is anything you need from me. I'm here to help in any way I can."

"Thank you so much," Ellie said as she rose and shook Ralston's hand. She left his office, safe deposit key in hand and headed for the bank.

Once inside the vault with the safe deposit box removed, the first thing Ellie noticed was the size of the box. It was one of the largest in the vault, and there weren't many of this size.

She assumed she would most likely find some important papers, maybe some old photographs or even some keepsakes from her parents. But as she lifted the lid, she was astonished to find a beautiful solid cherry box. When she looked inside, she found several black velvet boxes each housing a piece of extremely valuable jewelry.

Necklaces, bracelets, and rings all of precious stones in gold settings, of the utmost quality including diamonds, rubies, emeralds, and sapphires. She took one of the necklaces out of the velvet box, held it up cradling it in her hand. She recognized the quality and craftsmanship, not because she was an expert, but because she had seen pieces like this before.

Many of her clients had been given such pieces by their husbands, and these valuable jewels were always part of the divorce settlement.

After taking a few pictures of the jewelry with her cell phone, Ellie returned them to the velvet boxes, packed everything into the safe deposit box, rang the bell for the bank attendant, and left the bank. She was stunned by what she found but decided to head back to the house resolved to ask Ralston about it the next time they spoke.

Chapter Thirty One

Back at the house, she decided she would delve into searching through her grandmother's things. First, she went to the attic where she found several boxes with photographs, china, and glassware. More boxes had the usual stuff like Christmas decorations, old papers, and various knick knacks.

So far, everything seemed familiar given her recent trips to the house and the time she and her grandmother spent in the attic. There were also several pieces of old furniture, not in the greatest of condition and certainly of little value.

Just as she was about to return downstairs, she noticed a large crate at the far end of the room. It looked like one of the shipping crates typically loaded onto a cargo ship for transport on an ocean vessel. She was curious. The crate looked out of place, well built, new, and she wondered why her grandmother had placed this among all the other typical household items found in most family attics. She didn't remember seeing this crate on any of her previous visits.

She pried the top off the crate with a crowbar that she found nearby and, upon looking inside she was again surprised with what she found, artwork.... valuable artwork in a variety of mediums by different, but all famous artists. All she could think was, *What the hell is going on here?*

As she continued her search, she was astonished to find more valuable items and became increasingly curious about how and why they were here without her prior knowledge. She decided to contact her grandmother's lawyer.

"Hello, this is Ellie Gable. May I speak to Mr. Hayes?"

"Just one moment, Miss Gable, I will put you right through."

"Ellie, how are you?" Ralston asked.

"I'm doing fine. I'm just a little perplexed and hoping you can help explain something."

"What is it, Ellie? Is something wrong? Ralston asked.

"No. Nothing is really wrong, but I've been doing as instructed by my grandmother. First, I went to the bank to see the safe deposit box and found several extremely valuable pieces of jewelry inside. Then, in the attic at the house, I found a crate full of, valuable artwork."

She intended to continue, but he interjected, "are you sure they are of great value? I was unaware of her possessing such things."

"Yes." She stated with certainty. "I am quite sure. In my work as an attorney, I have represented many clients with wealthy husbands. In working to make sure they don't hide assets or lie about the true value, I have learned to recognize highly valuable assets. I've worked with some of the most respected appraisers in the country, and I'm sure, in total, these items are worth hundreds of thousands of dollars, and I haven't told you everything yet."

Ralston answered slowly, "Really…you mean there's more?"

Ellie went on, "In the canisters on the kitchen counter, I found the usual flour, sugar, coffee, and tea, but then there was a fifth which honesty I don't remember there being a fifth. In this one I found a set of rare coins, each one individually packaged and serialized. Then in one of the small, rundown garages at the back corner of the property, under an old tarp, I found a beautiful, fully restored antique car, I think it's a Rolls, not sure what year, but it's vintage. I recall my grandmother saying that the garage was unsafe and I shouldn't go in there, and as a kid, I never did. Why did she have all these valuable treasures hidden? Where did they all come from?"

"I'm just as surprised as you are, Ellie. I knew she was concerned about her wishes that you go over the property thoroughly, but that things of this magnitude would be found there, well that's just mind boggling and quite frankly, even a bit foolish on her part. These items should have been inventoried and insured. I just don't know what to say."

"I'm bewildered by this. I thought you would have some clue, but then you did say at our meeting that her estate wasn't complex. To think Eleanor didn't include these items specifically in her will, well it just doesn't make sense."

"I agree. Eleanor was well organized and prepared...I thought. For some reason, she didn't want me to detail these items in her will, but she was careful to make sure you found them."

Over the next several weeks, Ellie continued to search through the house and grounds and found more and more hidden treasures. Linda assisted her with the task of cataloging the items and getting formal appraisals including ensuring nothing had originated as stolen property. There didn't seem to be anything unusual, no clear patterns, and nothing that would lead to any illegal activity. This work, however, still did not answer the question for Ellie, how her grandmother came to own these items of value.

Once everything had been identified, they increased the insurance policy on the property and its contents. During this process, Ellie traveled between Atlanta and Tennessee juggling the demands of her growing law practice and settling things at her grandmother's house. Linda finished her paralegal program and with Ellie's training, gradually took on more responsibilities. They also hired a new administrative assistant.

As the first anniversary of her grandmother's death approached, she completed her search of the property and compilation of the items she found. Now, she had some decisions to make. She scheduled an appointment with her grandmother's lawyer.

"Mr. Hayes, I need to discuss a few things with you as we approach the anniversary of Eleanor's death. I've decided I want to do two things. First, I have decided to convince the police to reopen my parents' accident case. I must find out who was responsible for their deaths. Next, I have to understand where all of these treasures came from and why my grandmother hid them from me for all these years."

Ralston replied, "Oh Ellie, I completely understand your desire to learn these things, but are you sure you want to use your energy and time dredging up the sad case of your parent's deaths. I think it would be best if you move on with your life rather than digging up the past. Your grandmother must have had her reasons for what she did."

"No, I'm sorry, I can't let this go. Eleanor raised me, and I thought I knew her so well. We lived a quiet, simple life. She wasn't extravagant, taught me the value of a dollar, how to save, to live in moderation. And now, to find out she was sitting on such *wealth*.

Then there's my parents' death. I could never get her to talk about it, and I'm still confused about why she didn't seek justice. Why didn't she want the person responsible for their deaths identified and punished? I must find the answers, and I'm not going to rest until I do," Ellie stated with conviction.

"Is there nothing that will change your mind about this?"

"No. I will not stop until I find the truth!"

"You certainly are cut from the same cloth as Eleanor. You sound very much like her. I feel as if she is sitting here with me now."

He then rose from his desk chair, walked across his office to his wall safe, opened it, and removed a sealed envelope which he then handed to Ellie.

"This may give you some answers. I can't guarantee it, but I believe it might. Your grandmother entrusted me with this sealed envelope, never revealing its contents to me. She did say that if you pressed hard to find answers, specifically surrounding your parents' deaths, that I was to give you this. You are to read this in private and then destroy it immediately. Eleanor said you will understand once you have read it."

Part Four

Discovery

Chapter Thirty Two

"Hey Ronnie, how's it going?" Detective Burch asked as he entered the pawn shop.

"Not bad." He was casual in his speech as two customers were milling around the shop. He completed a sale with one and the other left after several more minutes of browsing. Ronnie then approached Detective Burch.

"What can I do for you, Burch? Want to have a seat out back, maybe have a cup of coffee or a nip?"

"Ronnie, I would love a drink. I'm just getting off duty and needed to stop by and give you some news. We need your services….again."

"Come on back. You look like you need some top shelf. How about a Makers Mark?"

"Sounds good." They both went through the archway behind the counter leading to the back room. Ronnie poured two doubles, and they sat at a small table to talk.

"So, what's up? Whatcha need?"

"Unfortunately, it's Arthur. He's getting a little nervous, and we may need to move him."

"What's got him nerved up?"

"A few hang-up calls, and he thinks someone may have been in his house. Arthur went away for an overnight after they dropped the charges in his case and arrested

Justin. When he got back, his alarm system was deactivated. He was sure he activated it when he left."

"Was anything in the house disturbed?"

"Not that he could tell, but putting that with the hang ups, and the fact that he doesn't have a job right now and he's not sure what to do next, he's unsettled. He's got some fear of being watched and then it's partly the need to do something different."

"You're not sure you want to move him yet, right? So what can I do to help?"

"No not yet, but we were hoping you could see if you can find any chatter about Arthur. We need to know if there could be a chance he's blown. There was a lot in the news about his arrest and pending trial. It wasn't very far-reaching, but you never know. It's so hard now with the internet, and unfortunately, pictures were taken and are out there."

"Got it. I'll do what I can and be in touch. Gonna put a detail on Arthur's house?"

"Yes, I think we have to. He's antsy, so the quicker we can make a decision on where to go from here, the better."

"Poor guy. I feel for him. He's been through it man and never asked for any of it."

"Yeah, me too. He's one of the good guys, not like most we work with, huh?"

"You got that right, Detective."

Chapter Thirty Three

"Hello, Ms. Virnetti?"

"Yes."

"This is Detective Burch." He paused giving her an opportunity to respond.

"Oh, yes, Detective Burch. I had to think for a moment. It's been a while since we've talked, and I'm surprised to hear from you."

"I understand. I was hoping we could meet. I have some information I want to share with you. It's about Arthur."

"Arthur, really?! I thought after the last time we spoke, I would never hear from you again. You seemed adamant that you would not be able to help me find him."

"That's true, but after further consideration and talking to the people I work with, the decision has been made to ....well... let's meet, and I will explain."

Layton was intrigued and suggested they meet right away. As she drove to the Sheriff's office, she wondered what he meant when he said the people he works with.

After stopping at the receptionist's desk to announce her arrival, Layton was brought to a small conference room to wait. She sat at the small table, tapping her fingers nervously until the door opened and Detective Burch and another man entered.

Detective Burch began, "Hello, Layton. My colleague is an agent with the FBI. He has some information to share with you and a document for you to read. He will explain."

The agent shook Layton's hand and then took a seat at the table. He set a single envelope on the table in front of him.

"I have something here for you to read. It's a letter from Arthur. After reading it, you must return it to me so that I can destroy it. The letter should answer your questions, but you are free to ask me anything before you leave. I have not read the letter."

He then passed the envelope to Layton. She opened it slowly, hoping the men would leave the room, but they remained.

Dear Layton,

I recently learned from my contact in the FBI that you've been trying to find me, and I wanted to write to first apologize for leaving without saying good-bye and then to explain. I'm not supposed to contact you, but given the circumstances, it was decided it would be possible for me to write to you with the condition that the letter be destroyed after you have read it.

Just before moving to your town, I provided evidence against the owner of the company I worked for who then struck a deal with the DA to avoid going to jail. He was able to give them what they needed to convict those guilty of more serious crimes, and we were both placed in the witness protection program. He was a criminal, I was not. Arthur Bowles is not my real name, but it was the name I lived with for the past several years. I have been relocated and have a new identity.

I remember when you asked me why I never married and didn't I want to have children. The truth is I had a wife and a child, but my wife died in an accident shortly before I went into the program. We had a little girl who my mother agreed to raise.

When I moved to your town, I was sad and afraid. I had to change my name, get a new identity, and a new job. I was afraid to associate with people because I didn't think I could pull it off. I was not good at being dishonest and thought people would know something wasn't right. You were the only one who treated me with kindness, and I was glad you never pressured me to reveal anything about my past, until the embezzlement charge. You can't imagine how lonely I would have been all those years without your friendship.

As you learned in your research preparing my defense, I was the anonymous donor that paid part of your tuition through law school. I remember the day you told me how excited you were to be able to attend. I was happy to help as I would have done for my own daughter.

I'm sorry I couldn't stay in Belmont, but Detective Burch and the FBI learned through some intelligence that someone was close to discovering my true identity and found it necessary to move me. It had to be done quickly with no warning, so I wasn't able to see you one last time.

I'll be able to learn about your life, but you will not be able to learn about mine. I'm sure mine will be uneventful as I will move to another town, have a modest job, and live somewhat in seclusion as I have before. I'm not complaining as I understand the necessity of my circumstances. I will always cherish the time I spent with you and find much joy in knowing I have had an impact on your life and success. That is enough for me.

You will remain in my heart,

Arthur

As she read the letter tears began to well in her eyes. When she finished, she paused in thought. *I hope that in his next town Arthur will cross paths with a young person with an open heart. One who will not make inaccurate assumptions about the quiet man, but will accept Arthur, or whoever he is now, just as he is.*

She then handed the letter over to the man and watched as he held it over an empty waste can and lit it on fire with his lighter. Detective Burch waited until the last shred of evidence burned into ash then turned to Layton and said, "I just want you to know that we're sorry we were unable to share information with you while you were representing Arthur, but it was necessary to protect Arthur as well as you. You can never reveal this information to anyone."

"I understand. Thank you for allowing Arthur to write to me, and the next time you're in contact with him, please let him know that I wish him well and miss him very much."

Detective Burch replied, "I won't be in contact with Arthur."

At which point he motioned with his hand to the other man in the room who responded, "I can let him know."

Detective Burch then said, "Thank you, Agent Breene."

Chapter Thirty Four

Ellie returned to her grandmother's house and opened the envelope she received from her grandmother's lawyer. Inside she found a letter in her grandmother's handwriting, and it read,

Dear Ellie,

If you are reading this letter, I know that Ralston has given it to you believing it was necessary. What I'm about to tell you may come as a shock, but it's imperative that you understand that everything I've done has been to protect you.

First, the accident. It is true, your parents were involved in a terrible accident coming home from the State Capital when you were very young, but it was no accident. Your father had turned state's evidence against the owner of the company he worked for, and he had also agreed to testify. Your family was going to be moved into the witness protection program. The car they were riding in was forced off the road, and your mother was seriously injured and would not survive. Your father's injuries were minor, not life threatening, and he would be treated and released. It was decided best to report that he was killed in the accident along with your mother.

He was so grief stricken by your mother's impending death, and he realized he would be putting you in danger if he brought you with him into the program. He made the most difficult decision of his life. He decided to let you grow up believing he was dead and he asked me to raise you and keep his secret.

In the program, he was relocated, given a new identity, training for a new profession and enough financial assistance to live for about a year. He could have no contact with anyone from his former life. I missed him so much and hated keeping this secret from you, but I had to keep you safe.

Now - the rest of the story. After a few years, on your seventh birthday, a package arrived. It was a bracelet in diamonds and gold. There was a small card inside that said "Happy Birthday".

I knew it was from him, and as time went on, I knew it was just the first step in his way of helping to secure your future. Every year after that on your birthday, something would arrive with the same printed card.

Over the years, I carefully hid the things he sent and continued to live as we had always lived so that there would be no attention drawn to us through our lifestyle. Then one year, your birthday came and passed with no delivery so I can only assume your father had died.

There was no way for us to know without contacting the FBI, and I didn't want to do that. I didn't want to reveal even to them what your father had been sending to us. I would suggest you assume the same and move on with your life.

Consider how you will use these gifts. You must be careful about directing any attention to yourself given who you are and your relationship to this man whose evidence helped put a lot of people in prison. Live discreetly and carefully, but of course, live happily as I know your father would want you to live.

I'm so sorry for the deception. I hope you will understand why your father and I kept this secret, for your protection, but also for his protection as well. Please destroy this letter now.

As always, I love you, Ellie!

Grandma El

In shock and disbelief, Ellie did as her grandmother instructed and burned the letter in the fireplace.

Chapter Thirty Five

As Ellie came to terms with what she had learned, she decided to give up her practice in Atlanta and move into her grandmother's house, her childhood home. She opened a new practice in Tennessee, this time focusing her cases on clients who were also victims of domestic violence, but of much lesser economic means. Now that she had inherited a fortune, she could afford to represent a majority of her clients for little or no legal fees.

Linda was willing to relocate as well. Her daughters had both married and were now living in different cities, providing no reason for Linda to stay in Atlanta.

Ellie would make a new life for herself without her beloved Grandma El. It was difficult, but she did understand why her father and grandmother made the choices they made to protect her. She only wished she could have seen her father, just once, having learned he had been alive for most of her life.

On her next birthday, she decided to close the office early and spend the afternoon shopping in town. Then she treated herself to a relaxing evening at home with a good book and a glass of wine. She wanted to be alone. She was not in any mood to celebrate.

As she sat comfortably in her favorite chair on the front porch, she put down her book and gazed out at the property. Her thoughts focused on birthdays past and how special Grandma El had made each and every one of them.

Just then, a local delivery truck drove up the long drive. After signing for the package, she opened it and found a signed, first edition of a novel she remembered reading as a teenager.

Inside the book was a small card. Ellie froze for a moment. The card dropped from her hand landing softly on the ground in front of her. The words imprinted on the card read:

Happy Birthday

Coming soon –

Finding William

By Kelly Lewis

Ellie Gable sat in her living room with a glass of Merlot in one hand and a small card in the other. The card read *Happy Birthday*. It was not signed. She had received the card one week earlier on her birthday, tucked into a book delivered to her door. The package had no return address. After seeing the card, she was in shock as it told her that the father she believed to be dead must be alive. She knew what she must do....she must find him.